If These Mountains Could Talk

By Emily Josabeth Klein

Dedicated to:

Alberto and Mari who love Cochoapa el Grande and its people, and to all the guys and families who worked hard, did good, and put their heart into the ministry; in honor of the times when we all ate dinner together and told stories.

To Santiago and Reina, as well as their daughter, for being hopeful lights in the darkness.

But most sweetly I dedicate this book to Lea, Modesto's little girl, in hope for the future.

Yet then from all my grief's, O Lord!

Thy mercy set me free,

Whilst in the confidence of prayer

My soul took hold of Thee.

In midst of dangers, fears, and death,

Thy goodness I'll adore

And praise Thee for thy mercies past,

And humbly hope for more.

-Joseph Addison

Chapter 1 – Just A Girl

Love has often been lacking in the heart of a man, but love never seems far from his vocabulary. Imagine then, a people in whose language the word 'love' does not exist. Is it lust that defines their affection? Surely there must be love in their hearts, but if so, it's still far from their mouths. Truly it's the only thing missing from their wondrous and complex language. *Mixteco* consists of tones, maybe somehow related to Chinese. But Mexico is far from China and the people who speak this variation of the Mixteco dialect are part of a small region in the south.

In this area, the mountains are sometimes soft and sometimes rugged, but they are all woven together and unified though each is a separate thread, like the native clothes that are still woven and worn in many places of the Sierra Madre del Sur. The mountains lie silently like great sleeping giants, unaware of the lives that live and breathe among them.

Despite the big tourist city, Acapulco, that it contains, the state of Guerrero in the southern end of Mexico, contains the poorest area in Mexico. Northeast of Acapulco and past the desert, the mountain tops stretch high in the cool crisp air, while the narrow valleys dig deep into the thick hot air. From the top to the bottom and all the layers in between, the mountains are speckled with tiny towns, connected by long, tan zigzags, tiny roads cut into the sides of the mountains.

Cochoapa el Grande – bigger than most of the small towns, as depicted by its name, stretches out on a long hill beneath three peaks, part of a mountain range that is immersed in cool air. The moist warm air from the coast meets the cool air on this range, producing a great deal of rain during the rainy season and heavy dew even in the dry season.

In this town, Rosalía Cordoba had her seventeenth birthday like she had all the others, but this one had put her uncle, with whom she lived, in a particularly bad mood.

"You're good for nothing!" he hollered in Mixteco as he paced across his small kitchen floor.

She stirred the pot on the fire, and flipped the tortillas on the big, round, clay *comal* over the fire. When babies are hungry they cry, when Tío is hungry he hollers, so a meal was the only hope for peace. Hope, it was, but not a guarantee. Rosalía squinted through the smoke, "I'm sorry, Tío, I try – " The smoke was beginning to sting her eyes as the wood under the comal began to burn faster.

"Stop saying that! You 'try', you 'try', and what do I

get? Nothing! All I get is my brother's kid to take care of. Just because of his silly, over-sensitive wife, I'm left with some girl that's burning my tortillas!" With that, he turned to his wife who had been sitting in the corner nursing the youngest of their children, "Go help the girl, woman."

Tía stood up, only halfway holding the baby who then started crying. With the unmoved and stiff expression she always had on her young face, Tía handed the baby to Rosalía and without a word took control of the pot, the comal, and the fire with skill that had been developed through years of experience. The smoke filled every corner of the room and hung still, seeping unnoticeably through the eaves and cracks in the walls.

The baby began to shriek in Rosalía's arms and she couldn't comfort her. "Help, help, help – that's all you need..." Tío mumbled.

The two children next in age – Teresa, age five, with

a constant runny nose, and Irvin, age nine, with a constant worried expression – were doing their grade school homework at the kitchen table. When Tío saw them, it inspired him and he turned to Rosalía again, "And that's another thing – you're stupid. You never learned nothing and it wasn't worth putting you in school."

Rosalía had put the wailing baby on her hip and with one arm was trying to flip tortillas for Tia. "Look at you," Tío continued, "You don't even have the brains to get yourself a husband. If you tried, maybe someone would take you, but ha," he laughed "he would have to be drunk or crazy." His flat nose wrinkled, "Ugly girl,"

Rosalía wasn't good at simply ignoring such an insult. Though she'd heard it before, every year it got louder, and every year it stung a little more. She knew better than to show that it hurt her, so she listened quietly and worked as best she could while holding the baby.

Tío finally sat down with a slump at the table. He kicked at the greasy-looking packed dirt floor still mumbling, his voice going from high to low and back to high again. His brown face was deeply creased with lines and his eyes had a faraway look in them that rarely made contact with the eyes around him. The lines in his face lightened for a moment as if inspired, "But you know why you don't try?" He said, "Because you've gotten other ideas from those Christians. Those city people and their church got you thinking about, what's the word they use?" He acted forgetful, "Oh yes, *amor*." He spit out the Spanish word, "Emotional girl – just like your mother."

His mockery accomplished its purpose. Her heart sank and her cheeks colored, she quickly grasped to defend herself, "It's not just an idea, it's the truth that God loves us"

"Now don't start that again!" He stood up straight and looked her up and down with big brown eyes hidden under messy eyebrows. Then he turned away as if totally disgusted with what he saw, "Ugly girl." he mumbled.

Throughout dinner he hardly spoke, but sat in the air of his superiority, looking over his small kingdom gathered together in the smoky kitchen. The two oldest of Rosalía's cousins had joined them and they too sat silent, the sounds of the fire and of baby Mari fussing, were the only sounds that dared interrupt the silence.

The sun set and the kitchen got dark except for the light of the fire under the comal and electric light from the adjoining room pouring from the cracks in between the boards of the wall. Paulina, the oldest of Rosalía's cousins, was sitting at the corner of the table where it was the darkest. The light flickered slightly over her pretty oval face.

In the distance music began to play loudly. It made no visible impression on anyone, except for a slight recollection on Tío's face, "You're going to the *baile*,

9

aren't you, Paulina?"

"Yes Papa," she said, her voice sweet and her eyes wide.

"Good," Tío said looking back at his plate, his face lightened with another burst of his previous inspiration. "You'd better not be like your cousin. Old maid and no good disposition. You go out, and are seen by people."

Rosalía saw Paulina smile to herself.

"But I warn you," Tío said and Paulina's smile disappeared, "You'd better be sure some man doesn't pick you up without giving me what you're worth."

"Of course, I wouldn't do that!" Paulina exclaimed a little too loudly.

Tío's gaze shot up to Paulina's face. His face had no particular expression but merely looking at her so directly was enough. Paulina tried to smile at her father, but quickly looked away. Tío finally looked away, but not before he mumbled, "I'll be there tonight anyway."

When he said this, Tia looked up at him cautiously,

but then looked down again without saying anything.

After dinner, Tío left and Paulina went into the adjoining room, the only other room in the house, which was about double the size of the kitchen and much nicer with a cement floor. Rosalía found her there a few moments later getting ready to go to the baile. Paulina was brushing her tremendously straight black hair when Rosalía sat down on the bed in front of her. Paulina picked up a bottle of baby oil from the little ledge on the wooden wall. She put some in her hands and then spread it through her hair, then pulled her hair back into a slick pony tail that fell below her waist.

"Now," Paulina said, her neck gracefully arched, "should I go with the traditional look or with the modern one?" She pulled the ruffled skirt and woven *huipil* from the rope that hung across the room on which the family hung their clothes. She had hints of a very young beauty in her face, hints of innocence being outnumbered by a willful decisiveness of knowledge. She looked at the woven cloth of the long shirt-like huipil with its flowers and figures of animals and at the neon-colored ruffles and ribbons of the skirt, then tossed it over the rope again. "I'm not a grandma." She looked down at her slightly tight jeans and shirt, and then grinned at Rosalia.

She didn't return the grin. She glanced down at her own huipil that she always wore. She was fond of the yellow ribbons, blue deer and yellow flowers that she had woven herself. Her light purple skirt was simple and worn, but she loved that color. Paulina let out a sigh and sat down next to her. "Are you sure you don't want to go with me, Rosalia?"

Rosalia shook her head, "No. You know I don't like what goes on at those things."

"What goes on 'at those things' is getting a husband!" Paulina exclaimed rather suddenly and nudged Rosalia. Again, she didn't respond. Paulina looked at her and Rosalia could tell she was genuinely concerned. "If someone would buy you, my dad wouldn't be so upset. You're seventeen years old now, Rosalia, and still not married. My dad is afraid you'll still not be married by the time you're eighteen and he'll lose half of the money he wants whenever you do marry. You have a year before the amount is cut in half. Make the most of that year. Take me, for example, I'm only fifteen, but I'm out looking. You should do the same." She spoke softly, giving her best advice, "Besides," she whispered close to Rosalia's ear, like a child would, "maybe if a man really liked you, he would just run away with you and not even bother with all that paying stuff. What's wrong," she turned Rosalia's face toward hers, "don't you like men?" She didn't wait for an answer, instead, she giggled, stood up, and continued, "But the way you are, with your wild hair and personality, no one wants to buy you, much less do something so romantic like run away with you." She checked herself in the little mirror hung on the board wall, then looked at Rosalía for a moment, "But you wouldn't run away, would you? It would be against your new religion." She sighed and when Rosalía again said nothing, Paulina left.

Rosalía sat alone on the hard bed. It wasn't religion – she detested the use of that word – and it wasn't new, she had been a Christian for five years now. Yet it seemed that those were the only things she was sure of. Did she like men? She wasn't sure she did. Would she run away if she had the opportunity? She hadn't thought of it.

In a few minutes, Tía came in; Rosalía was still numbly staring into space, wondering if she was the only sane one, or the only insane one. When Rosalía saw her aunt come in, she smiled at her weakly. Tía didn't care what kind of smile it was, she ignored it and sat down on her own bed with the baby in her arms.

Rosalía sighed, "Paulina is being foolish."

"Don't talk so daringly." Tía said, looking at her stalely, "Your mouth will get you in trouble."

Rosalía pressed her lips together for a moment, but she was tired of being silent, "Tía, this is not the way God intended things to be. God is love and he meant for people to fall in love and not just go buy a wife."

"That sounds sweet, but it's not reality. At least, not for us. It never has been."

"Buying and selling girls isn't right – it never has been."

Tía seemed shocked for a moment, "Who are you to say that?" Then she looked down at the baby in her arms. Her cold, unaffectionate eyes were stripped down to a simple sadness as she looked at her child, but when she spoke her voice was still unchanged, "You are just a girl, good for nothing but to please a man; to make his tortillas and give him children. You don't have a choice and you never will." She looked away from Mari and away from Rosalía and seemed to be talking to the wall before her, "It's time you face reality. You are being foolish, not Paulina."

Rosalia had stood up and was now looking into the small mirror. She fixed her eyes on herself. She was so different from Paulina. Her complexion wasn't the shiny, yellowish tan of most, but like dark brown sand. Her face, eyes, nose, and lips seemed to match in roundness; eyes a vibrant brown and lips only faintly pink. But what made her particularly different from the others was her thick, long black hair that curled itself into thousands of little curls. Her neck wasn't graceful and any hints of personality that could have been in her face lay dormant under an over-all quietness.

She looked away, "Reality." she mumbled. She stooped down and pulled a little wooden crate out from under the bed. She took from it a paper-back Bible. It was dirty and its cover was curling, but she held it carefully and made her way out of the house.

The house was on a small hill on the higher end of

the town. A steep trail went down from the house to the street. The top of a street light was nearly level with the house. It was under the streetlight on the edge of the hill that she sat down with the Bible in her lap. She opened the Bible but didn't read it, instead she looked down the main street. The yellow tarp of the *baile* was spread across the main street like a tent, under it in the dim light she could see the people.

Most of the people were standing around at the edges of the tent, and only a handful of people were in the middle, their figures stumbling and bouncing pitifully mimicking the bounce of the music.

The music, though truly unfit to be called so, was not only bouncy but redundant – a rhythm with no beauty. But this meaningless tune still echoed through the mountains, hills, and valleys, and the sound of it falling off the side of mountains was far more beautiful than the music itself. It made the world sound so much bigger than it could look, even from the tops of mountains.

This was why Rosalía didn't read her Bible that night. The contemplation of the bigness of the rest of the world and the smallness of her own consumed her thoughts. She could hear the rest of the world, but she couldn't see it.

It was late when Paulina came back. Rosalía was only half asleep when she heard Paulina stumble into the room. Paulina slipped into bed next to Rosalía and with that, the smell reached Rosalía: a slight smell of fireworks smoke and an overpowering smell of beer. Rosalía was now wide awake. "You're late." she whispered.

"I have no time limit." Paulina whispered and Rosalía wrinkled her nose, "Oh, it was amazing," Paulina went on as if she had been asked. "I don't think I'll be hanging around here much longer. I saw Leo. He's so handsome and tall. I think he likes me. I won't be surprised if he wants to run away with me. He wouldn't have to force me, not at all. Any day now I'll be driving away with him in his Nissan truck – he owns it, you know." Her breathing got heavier as she began to doze off to sleep in half delirious contentment. "Any day now..." she slurred lastly.

Though the smell on Paulina was nauseating, and her words were mumbled and slurred, they seemed to be pronounced with such arrogance. It was the arrogance of someone who knew what to do with her life and knew how to do it. It left Rosalia completely aware of the fact that she was an orphan with no plans and dreams of things that could ever be reality.

She rolled over attempting to get away from the smell asleep next to her. She tried to think about how good it felt to be loved by God, but she couldn't concentrate on anything other than the truth of her reality. She stared at the dark board wall in front of her, she knew this all too well, she knew what mood came next in the cycle. A melancholy mood would overcome her, then that would be taken over by worse feelings – ones of doubt, fear, and regret. She closed her eyes and tried to pray but her mind was empty. She searched for words. She had to trust that God was there, loved her, had thrown all her sins into the depths of the sea, and wouldn't let these things become her life. She hoped her family wasn't right, she prayed her family wasn't right. She was tired of the worry and the present that was dragging into the future.

Her prayers were short and sounded more as if she were talking to herself. She soon fell asleep.

Her dreams were a confusion of pictures and stories, just like her thoughts had been a confusion of rights and wrongs.

When she awoke everything was still dark, but she knew it was time for her to begin the daily work. The sky to the east had a tiny hint of gray when she went outside to wash her face in the cold water.

The day began like any other, and part of Rosalía hoped it would be like all the others, yet she dreaded another day like all the others. Only one thing she knew for sure, a young girl still asleep inside had hope that the day would be the beginning of something new.

Chapter 2 – Reality

The sun was high when a scream pierced the air. Rosalía ran around to the front of the house and immediately saw a man holding Paulina by the arm, trying to pull her away. Paulina struggled free and ran to her. She caught hold of the bottom of Rosalía's *huipil* and clutched it with both of her hands. Stooped and breathing quickly, she looked up at Rosalía, "This isn't what was supposed to happen." Her eyes filled with tears and her face twisted in desperation, "Leo was supposed to want me – not Santiago."

She had hardly pronounced his name when

Santiago caught Paulina by her arm again. Paulina started to break lose when her father caught her other arm. She didn't scream, and she didn't cry, she only starred at Rosalía breathing quickly as if her lungs wouldn't fill with air.

Santiago starred at Rosalía for a moment as well. His eyes were smiling, but his mouth hung open lazily.

The instant was over and all eyes left Rosalía as Tío and Santiago led Paulina down the hill to the street. When they got to the bottom of the hill, Tío let go of his daughter's arm and she no longer struggled. Rosalía could see her shoulders were bent and shaking, but no longer struggling. She realized that in those few minutes Paulina had come face to face with reality and had accepted it like the women around her had done for countless generations. Would she eventually have to face reality in a few short minutes like Paulina had?

When they had heard the scream, everyone had come out of the house. Tia had watched her eldest daughter be taken away against her will, as her youngest daughter clung to her, but her face was still unmoved. Teresa – still too young to accept the realities of life – was sobbing and Irvin's face was twisted in trying to accept them. Manuel, however, was leaning against the wall, his face expressionless and unmoved like that of his mother. He, the oldest male, was the only one of the children left that didn't seem surprised.

They stood quietly as Paulina walked down the street held by the arm by her new husband. She walked slowly, and her husband pulled her to walk faster. She stopped and they could hear her voice far away screech at him, "I'm going with you; you don't have to pull me!" Santiago's arm flew up and she immediately began to walk faster. They were soon out of sight.

Tío had come up the hill again, a smile on his face. He went to his wife who handed him a bag she had been holding for him. He took it and looked at Rosalía, who looked away.

"Well," she heard Manuel mumble, "it finally happened." He sounded more relieved than upset. Without another word, he turned away and shuffled away down the hill with his hands in his pockets. No one said anything to him and he left for unknown places, not to be seen again until dinner time.

Teresa ran inside, not comforted by anyone, and Irvin wandered away. Rosalía was about to go back to her work, but as she passed Tío, he stopped her, "You're going to have to work harder now that Paulina's gone."

"Yes, Tío."

"Right now, go to the market." He handed her a clean one-hundred-peso bill out of the bag and listed the things he wanted her to buy.

She took the bill and made her way to the center of town. She knew where the money came from and she couldn't help but feel she had a part of her cousin's whole existence in the palm of her hand. It made her suddenly angry. She stopped and looked down at the red-colored bill in her hand. After observing the face of Nesauacoyolt for a moment, she crumpled it in her fist, and then looked at her fist for a moment, then continued walking down the street with the red-faced Nezauacoyolt crushed between her fingers.

She walked on the dusty unpaved streets and made her way past the board houses and little stores to the center of the town by the Catholic Church where the tiny stands made up the market place. She spent the crushed bill and started to make her way back.

Half way home, she went down a side street and knocked on a large, neatly cut wooden door. The door swung open a few seconds later, and a man stood there. He smiled widely, "Rosalia! How are you?"

She hesitated then managed a small smile, "I'm all right Gregorio, but Paulina has been sold." She looked down more in shyness than in sadness, being embarrassed to talk about these things, especially to Gregorio and not his wife.

Gregorio gasped, a little more dramatically than Rosalia had expected. Like a wind, Gregorio's wife, Vero, appeared behind him, rushed passed him, and wrapped Rosalia up in a big hug. She could feel Vero's long earrings making dents in the side of her face as Vero spoke what was meant to be words of comfort. She heard very little of what Vero said, but she heard Gregorio mumble as he leaned against the closed door, "These people..." He put a hand partly over his face, but she saw the deep wrinkles form in his forehead.

"I've got to go now," she said, pulling away from Vero. They nodded and smiled sad smiles. She didn't understand why they smiled, so she just nodded and left. They appeared so much sadder than Rosalia felt at that moment. Their eyes were sad, yes, but more than that she saw an appearance of panic in them.

Gregorio and Vero had come to Cochoapa el Grande when Rosalia was still a little girl and even then, she knew that despite all other rumors, the reason Gregorio and Vero had moved there from the city was to help the Indian people. She had supposed it was only because they felt sorry for them, and sometimes it didn't feel good to be felt sorry for. When they first came, she remembered, that though she was still a child, she didn't like being pitied. She resented all the missionary's giving, but she never hesitated to take all she could when they gave it. She was the child that took freely and never said thank you. She hated being called poor and considered ignorant. But the time came for her when she realized why Gregorio and Vero were really there. It wasn't because they felt sorry, because a feeling by itself would have worn away with all that time and no results. It wasn't a feeling alone, but something greater than feeling brought them there, and it was that which brought panic in their eyes and wrinkles on their faces.

Other than a little extra work, nothing had really changed. Or so it seemed, until that night when the work was done and Rosalía was free to think.

27

She sat in the usual spot under the street light with her Bible in her hand – again, not reading it. Of course, she was sad. Paulina had been like her sister; their childhood had been spent together. She remembered how she and Paulina would go together to the lunches that the missionaries would give the kids after school, and how they would go to the church to play and to see if they would give them something. As they got older Paulina got interested in boys, but Rosalía didn't stop going to church. Until then, she and Paulina had been best friends. For a moment, she thought maybe it was her fault – she should have tried harder to help Paulina, but the moment slipped away. She knew who to blame. It was Tío's fault, and Santiago's fault. It was the fault of men, and the fault of the culture they lived in. She passed this thought through her mind again and again as she looked out over the town. The more she looked at the town and thought about her world, the angrier her thoughts became.

That night she lay down on her bed, now shared by Teresa. After everyone had gone to sleep, the room was quiet, with only the sounds of sleeping people inside and the sounds of a half-sleeping village outside. There weren't any smells other than the musty smell of the little girl next to her.

She tried not to think about Paulina, but there was nothing else to think about. She imagined how Paulina must feel at this moment, but no, she didn't want to imagine Paulina at this moment. The more she thought, the more she didn't want to think. It was all the men's fault, wasn't it? Or was it also Paulina's fault? She did just want this, didn't she? But not like this. She had just wanted happiness like everyone else does, but the only ones that end up happy are the men.

The same ending is inevitable for me, she thought, *even though I don't go chasing guys doesn't mean no one will ever want me and take me. Someday one will.* The thought of a man wanting her was a terror, a bad dream she could only wish to escape. The more she thought of this, the worse her fear got. She had heard of people that married for love, but who was she to wish for something like that? She wasn't rich or beautiful or in any position of power in which a respectable man would ceremoniously buy her, and she wasn't sure that even a respectable man could gain her affection. Romantic love wasn't a reality for her. The reality of life pounded in her ears that night, as her heart pounded restlessly.

Out of pure fatigue she slept, but this new panic was in her sleep, and though she wished to wake from her dreams, she couldn't.

The panic was a dull ache in her stomach when she woke, still tired, the next morning. She got up and went outside. She went to the rectangular cement sink called a *lavadero* and dipped some cold water from the open barrel next to it as the water splashed into it from a black hose that usually hung across the road to their house. She washed her face. The clouds were still lying lazily in the lower hills. As the sun rose, they rose as well, unveiling the smoky mountains of the dry season. Those mountains: they were the only thing in the way of her and the rest of the world, the only thing in the way of a better life. If only she could get away from this place.

Days and nights passed. In the day, her thoughts rushed through her head as if they were in a hurry, and at night they slowed down enough to sit and weigh heavily on her. Her mind dwelt on her worry with persistence, and as it grew it had no choice but to turn into dull, hopeless anxiety.

One night, as she lay next to Teresa, she was tired of worrying. She put her face into her flat pillow. She closed her eyes and mouthed words but made no sound, "Lord," she mouthed, "My heart is sore. I just want to go away. Don't You see what will happen if I don't?" Her eyes were closed so tightly that tears couldn't escape her eyes, "Don't you see?" Her throat got tight, "Get me out of here – please. I know You don't want that to happen to me, I know You would never want me to go through that. I trust You, and You have to get me out of here."

A sob finally broke from her tight throat, and Teresa moaned. Rosalía sucked in her breath and held it. Once it was quiet again, she let out her breath, but she couldn't think of anything more to pray. The ache hadn't gone away, so she closed her eyes and fell asleep uncomforted.

She woke up the next morning and she knew what she was going to do. She had to leave, and if God wouldn't help her, she would just have to do it herself. She would run away to some big city, probably Mexico City or Acapulco, and work as a maid. She would leave during the planting of the corn. Tio would be gone for a few days working in his corn fields, so he wouldn't notice for a while. Since she was trusted, it would be easy to run away without anyone following her. Most likely no one would. Her uncle always said he just wanted to get rid of her, didn't he? There was just one problem: where would she get money to run away?

She thought about how to get the money as the day passed. She couldn't make enough money by working, even if she could get some sort of job. There was the money Tío had gotten for Paulina. What was he going to do with it anyway? But he wouldn't give any of it to her. Where did he keep it? But no, that would be stealing. No, the only people that would loan her the money would be Gregorio and Vero. That night was the Wednesday night meeting, she would ask them for the money after the meeting – but she couldn't tell them what it was for.

She walked down the road to Gregorio and Vero's house as the sun was beginning to set. She was trying to think of what she would tell them the money was for.

33

She was trying to think of a way to not tell them a lie but not tell them the truth either.

She arrived at their house but didn't knock on the door like she had before; instead she went across the patch of bare ground where they parked their truck, to a small wall-less building where people had begun to gather. She didn't speak to anyone, instead quickly took a seat.

The meeting started but she couldn't concentrate on it. She was trying to decide on what to tell them about the money, then she began daydreaming of what she would do once she was away from there. She would go to Acapulco first, she so wanted to see the ocean, then maybe after some time there, she would go to some of those big cities to the north. Maybe someday she would make it as far as those places where the land is flat and there would be no more mountains to contain her.

But what if she didn't get the money? Or even if she did, would it be that great? Out in the city, she probably couldn't make enough money to do anything. Would it be worth it? All these questions nagged at her, despite her daydreams, and one stood out beyond the others: Would this really be what God wanted for her life? She tried to put that thought out of her mind because surely freedom is what God wants for everyone.

In spite of all her thinking, she did eventually begin to listen to Gregorio's sermon. The story had caught her attention. It was about King Saul in the Old Testament. The Philistines had gathered against Israel and the people were afraid, but Saul waited for the prophet Samuel.

"*Then he waited seven days, according to the time set by Samuel. But Samuel did not come to Gilgal; and the people were scattered from him. So, Saul said, "Bring a burnt offering and peace offerings here to me." And he offered the burnt offering. Now it happened, as soon as he had finished presenting the burnt offering, that Samuel came...*" Gregorio read the verses slowly, and then he looked up from his Bible to the faces of the people, "Sometimes all God wants us to do is wait for Him. And we could be like Saul. He felt he had to do something, anything, and why couldn't he do what Samuel normally did? What harm could it do? But here we see in 1 Samuel 13:13-14, exactly what harm this did for King Saul. *"And Samuel said to Saul, you have done foolishly. You have not kept the commandment of the Lord your God, which He commanded you. For now, the Lord would have established your kingdom over Israel forever. But now your kingdom shall not continue. The Lord has sought for Himself a man after His own heart, and the Lord has commanded him to be commander over His people, because you have not kept what the Lord commanded you.'* We see that God says that his kingdom would have been forever." He paused, "Would have been. But he lost it all because he did not wait when God told him to wait. No, he felt he had to do something even though God never told him to do it."

At some point her thoughts had abandoned her. She hesitated because of what this could mean for her current plan. Surely God didn't mean that He wanted her to be bought; maybe He just meant that He wanted her to wait. Her excuses were useless when she realized what Gregorio – what the Bible – was saying.

Gregorio continued, "But what the Bible says to those who wait is very different. Isaiah 40:31 says, *'But those who wait on the Lord shall renew their strength; They shall mount up on wings like eagles, they shall run and not be weary, they shall walk and not faint.'"*

Wait. It didn't seem like a command, but a hand that was reaching to stop her with the simple reason of, 'wait'. It was right and though she didn't want to accept it, something in her just had to. Maybe the words were just so beautiful, or maybe they were just so real. Maybe she was crazy, but maybe not all this was in her hands anyway. Maybe God really did have plans and she just needed to wait for them. Her thoughts were crowded and a large part of her didn't want to wait – but she was struck with the realization that what she decided at this moment would change her whole future. She didn't want her future to be the same as all the others in her town – but yet – a future without the guidance and blessing of God would be no future worth living. She remembered how she had once known without a doubt that God is good.

As Gregorio finished his sermon and the people began singing their final song, it seemed as though God had put a simple question before her: *Do you trust me?* And as they bowed their heads and prayed she couldn't think of the words to answer. She knew it wasn't the kind of question that was answerable with words, only action could answer it.

In all of this, the panic had disappeared and as the meeting ended, she had made her decision.

She made her way to Gregorio and Vero as the people began to leave.

"Rosalia!" Vero reached to hug her.

"How are you?" Gregorio said, his face serious.

"I'm better now, I think."

Vero smiled a sad smile, and Gregorio looked at her closely, "We're praying for you." Vero said.

"Thank you." she answered simply, then turned to leave.

She walked home in the dust as the sun was setting – red in the smoke of the mountains being burned for the year's planting. The fields on the mountains were black and the trees around them were red and dying from fires that had gotten away from the fields and spread to the forest.

Her walk was lighter now because she didn't carry with her the weight of worry. There was no logic in her peace, the problem hadn't gone away, and nothing had changed, only now she wasn't the one in charge of the worry. She wasn't bursting with happiness, but she had peace and the peace of God is greater than all happiness.

That night, under the street light, she whispered in the night air. "Have I resigned myself to a life of misery? Is a decision to wait and trust not wise? Oh God, this isn't easy – but I suppose that bravery is never easy, and trust is never easy, and even hope isn't easy. I don't have hardly any of these things: bravery, hope, or trust in You, but I want to. I'm sorry for giving up on You. I know you never have given up on me before – please, never give up on me because I can't do this alone." The dew had fallen as the night had, and it could be heard dripping, every so often, from the tin roof. "I trust You," she whispered finally.

She went into the kitchen and found it empty. In the dim light of the red coals of the dying fire, Rosalia read Psalm 32:10 "Many sorrows shall be to the wicked; but he who trusts in the Lord, mercy shall surround him."

"Yes, I know the world I live in, but I also know the God I believe in. This is your strength, not mine."

She slept that night in peace and the days seemed to carry on as they always had. Her home was still her home, her work was still her work, and her family was still her family. But she lived differently. Her dreams of faraway places stayed as far away as those places. She wasn't always happy, hopeful or free from worry, but she had again remembered that God cared and she made a decision that she had to continue making every day – a decision to trust God, and be content with Him.

Chapter 3 – What's Important in Life

"*Amor vincit omnia*," the priest mumbled, a natural expression on his young face, he lifted his arms ceremoniously. He was handsome, capable of turning young girl's heads until they realized he was a priest by his high collared black robe which he always wore. He seemed but one spot at the front of the church where a giant image of the virgin of Guadalupe looked down sadly at the priest. The least he could do was speak up, even if what he was saying was in Latin. Sebastian's eyes floated shut and then jerked back open again. His mother nudged him. He sat straight up again and tried to look interested. He looked sheepishly around the church to see if anyone else was paying attention.

His father, as always, was attentive. He seemed more attentive to what the priest said than the priest was to his own words. He sat with his chest puffed out and hanging on every Latin word that came from the priest's mouth. His father's hair was a wild mop of gray that he kept slicked back neatly. His eyes were narrow and attentive, but dominantly disapproving. His eyes sliced the air as he looked up at the priest. He didn't respect the priest, he only approved of him, which was more than he did of anyone else.

His mother was at attention, but yet, he knew she was thoroughly disinterested in what was being said. He knew his mother. She wasn't so strictly religious like his dad, but she loved to please him, so she played like she was. For her, church was more of a social choice. "All successful people go to church to see and to be seen." she would say. She ran her fingers through her dyed-blond hair and admired her rings and nails. *To see and be seen,* Sebastian thought, stifling another yawn.

The priest switched to Spanish, but Sebastian didn't notice. His head was making its way back to a hanging position. A strong pinch from his mother's long manicured nails snapped him straight again. He looked up to the high ceiling where a painted eye stared at him. He shuddered, *Creepy eyeball,* he thought.

His younger brother, far from sleeping, but also far from listening, sat next to Sebastian on the aisle, leaning partly into it and smiling at a girl a few rows up. His wild eyes were laughing and his lips were curled into a flirtatious smile. Oscar always had a girl, though he was never considered a heartbreaker, at least not by himself. He said he always broke off with his various girls as friends, though some of the girls wouldn't agree with that statement. He carried with him quite a record, though he had only just graduated from high-school that summer, and he carried with him great hopes for the university. He had only recently decided what to study, but that's not what he looked forward to. A young man like Oscar didn't go to the university to study.

His mother looked accusingly at Oscar. Sebastian was the only thing in the way from her grabbing a lock of his hair or an ear and giving it a strong yank so he would stop making eyes at every girl in church. She quietly slipped her arm around Sebastian and got ahold of one of Oscar's ears. She yanked it as she silently looked ahead at the priest. Oscar, however, wasn't so silent about it. He gave out a little yelp that woke Sebastian up again, made the girls Oscar had been smiling at burst into giggles, and made their father look at them all with his beady, harsh eyes.

Even when the recitation started, the mass seemed

to last forever to Sebastian, and nothing more interesting happened. Oscar rubbed his ear the rest of the time, and Sebastian suffered through his mother's pokes and pinches.

When it was time to leave, he stood up stiffly, and proceeded slowly behind his mother who walked with her head high, giving smiles graciously and greetings to the important people. Leaving seemed to take longer than everything else. He looked up at the few high stained-glass windows seeing the bright Acapulco sun shinning brilliantly through them. They were the most bright and beautiful things in the church. Along the walls near the pews, where the Arroyo's were seen walking slowly in the company of their friends, there were little show-cases of Jesus hanging on the cross or lying dead. They struck Sebastian as being very sad scenes, so he ignored them.

Finally stepping outside he took a deep breath, realizing as he filled his lungs with warm ocean air, how much the church smelt unbearably of incense. Now outside, the girls took advantage of Oscar's pulled ear as they 'rubbed it to make it feel better', and he basked in their attention.

After a while of ear rubbing, one girl seemed to get bored of it and wandered over to where Sebastian was standing with the adults. "Hello, Sebas," Fatima said, "How are you?" She formed every word with her red lips working to move as much as they could while saying as little as possible. She blinked her long lashes and stood in a way that would bring the most attention to her tight, little dress.

Sebastian nodded in recognition of her and went on listening to the adult's conversation.

"How goes the primary elections, Draco?" Fatima's father asked Sebastian's father.

"Going well, Bruno, I have a good feeling about becoming the candidate." Draco Arroyo smiled proudly and puffed out his chest.

"I understand that hiring people to campaign for these kinds of things can be quite expensive. Or do you plan to do it all yourself?" Bruno laughed.

"Do you think I would do that?" Draco's laugh burst out loudly and deeply. "Of course, I will do the major cities and such. No, my sons will help with the smaller places since Sebastian is home from the university and Oscar has graduated."

"But Draco, there are a lot of Indian villages in this state, are they going to those as well?"

"Yes, they will Bruno! If I'm going to be the candidate for the PRD, I'm going to need all the votes I can get. And that includes the ignorant, uncivilized of this state. I understand they are some of the easiest people to convince, you throw some food at them and they vote for you."

They found the last remark quite funny and all the adults laughed.

"How's the university Sebas?" Fatima cut in, making

47

him jump.

He realized it was only her, so he pressed his lips tightly together and smiled as best he could. "It's going good." His voice had the loud quality of his father, but it rang out in crispness, not depth. He stepped back from her large blinking eyes and sour face. She stepped closer to his and batted her lashes again. "Two years more and I'll be a full-fledged lawyer," he said, trying to sound older than her, and trying to talk to her and avoid her at the same time.

"Awe, you're much too handsome to be a lawyer," she nearly whispered to him. He stepped away from her, concealing a look of disgust with a look of arrogance.

"Hey! That's what you told me!" Oscar said, showing up behind them and pulling them away from the adults to the group of college students, newly graduated high-school students, and the few high school kids that dared hang around with the older crowd.

Fatima laughed, "I know Oscarito, and you have

taken my advice. Business management is much more exciting and less strenuous than being a lawyer. Lawyers get stuck in offices doing paper work." She put a pouty look on her face and then took it off and giggled at Oscar, pulling his ear, and then in the same moment glanced at Sebastian. She went on giggling with Oscar, but was constantly checking back on Sebastian.

Sebastian didn't avoid her glances, he would simply stare back at her until she looked away again. She really bored him. It wasn't that she was bad looking, she simply wasn't good enough for him. She was a child in her attitudes, she had no right to tell him what to do with his time.

They had been standing across the street from the Catholic Church, under the trees of a small park near to where their cars were parked. Soon, the group broke up and Sebastian's mother, Drusilla, invited Bruno's family to eat with them.

Mass had been early for them, and none of them had eaten breakfast yet, so at about noon they arrived at one of their favorite cafés on the beach of the city of Acapulco.

The sun glistened off the blue Pacific Ocean and a sea breeze carried the warm, salty smell of the water across the sandy beach and across the boardwalk. Both families gathered on the wooden boardwalk in front of the restaurant, about ten yards from the water's edge. Standing by round tables beneath large umbrellas, they looked out at the ocean as they listened to the live music coming from band inside the restaurant. They had a waiter put two of the round tables together and when they settled around them, Fatima maneuvered herself into a seat between Sebastian and Oscar.

The head waiter's eyes lit up when he saw them arrive, and he came to them and slightly bowed in respect to Draco Arroyo, "What can I get you to drink this lovely day, Señor Arroyo?" He said, lowering his eyes and listening intently.

Draco leaned back, pleased, and waved his hand at everyone at his table. They all looked down at their menus, as Draco turned to the waiter, "Bring me my usual."

"I'll have a beer." Oscar said and slammed down his menu and smiled.

"Bring me one too." Sebastian said less dramatically than his brother did.

Fatima smiled and ordered a piña colada, her parents ordered similarly, and Drusilla quietly ordered a bottle of water.

"Ah, being healthy, are we?" Fatima's mother exclaimed.

Drusilla nodded as Draco answered, "Well, if she's going to be the governor's wife, she can't be flabby, now can she?"

That led to the married women discussing diets and health solutions. Health and diet were Fatima's mother's favorite hobbies.

"Oh!" Fatima exclaimed to the men seated beside her, "Renata is having a party at her place tonight." She put a hand on each of the guy's shoulders, "You had better come or you will disappoint so many of us," she turned to Sebastian, "especially me." He felt her squeeze his arm lightly.

"Sure, Fati," Oscar grinned and reached for her hand. She laughed and let him hold her hand.

Oscar had been looking out on the beach and in a few moments, he let go of her hand and leaned back to talk to his brother, "Hey, Sebas, look at those girls out there." He let out a low but shrill whistle and everyone at the table looked to see what Oscar was seeing. The wives nudged their husbands, and Fatima looked down, being suddenly very interested in her nails.

Oscar mumbled something to Sebastian and they both laughed. He continued looking out at the people on the beach, then he began to laugh, and he pointed, "Oh man, look at those people."

Sebastian looked and saw an old couple in long-sleeved shirts, floppy hats, and with sunscreen on their noses. "Oh, yeah, definitely tourists." Sebastian laughed.

As all this occurred, Fatima's mother had been observing Oscar, when she finally interrupted their laughter, "You have an eye for beautiful women don't you, Oscar?"

"That I do!" Oscar said without hesitating.

Everyone laughed, but then Sebastian turned to Oscar with the keen seriousness of his father on his face, "You know, Oscar, women aren't the most important thing in life."

Fatima snuck a curious look at Sebastian.

"What's important in life is a good education." he said.

"Sure," Oscar grinned, "What's most important in life is education, but what's most fun in life is women."

"Well, you have a point there." Sebastian grinned slightly, and Fatima smiled at him.

Oscar was on his third beer when Fatima's family left. As she left, he shouted out his promise that he would go to Renata's party that night, but that he couldn't promise that his stuffy brother would be there too.

When they were out of sight, Sebastian turned to Oscar, "Stuffy? Seriously? You know very well the reason I'm not going to that party, tonight of all nights. We're leaving early tomorrow to work on dad's campaign."

"Oh, would you relax? It's just one party; it'll probably end before midnight and everything."

"Any other time that would be fine, but we've got a job to do and we have to be sharp. We have a job to do" he repeated," and that must take priority, no parties, no girls, no nothing until we're done."

"Eh, you just don't want to go because Fatima's after you and you don't like her."

"Would you grow up, Oscar?"

Oscar didn't answer, and Sebastian was left looking at his brother, and still waiting for a response.

"Calm down, Sebastian." His mother whispered to him, putting her hand on his arm. She stood up, "Will you walk with me?"

He got up and his mother took his arm. They walked out on the wooden sidewalk over the sand. "Your brother doesn't think like you do yet." his mother said, looking up at him from behind her sunglasses, "He's not as mature as you are. In time, he'll learn what's worth his time and what's not, but right now he feels the need to waste time. We must let him."

She held on to his arm gently, and he listened but did not respond.

"Why aren't you nice to Fatima?" she asked a few moments later.

"Well, I don't know. I guess I like to watch her get frustrated. She's so obvious, it's sickening."

"Son, don't just play with her feelings. You're just letting her down. If you played your cards right with her, you could have a girlfriend. Or is it just because you have your eye on a girl at school? I really wish you would tell me these things. I'd like to meet her – I don't think it would be wise not to tell your father and have him hear it from someone else. We are becoming a very important family. We can't afford any kind of scandal, even of the smallest degree."

"No – Mama – it's nothing like that. There are a few girls there, but I'm really just concentrating on school right now. I don't need a girlfriend, and honestly, I'm tired of playing around with girls. At this point, I want something serious or nothing at all, and I think nothing at all is better. And Fatima just wants to play, so she gets on my nerves."

"Well, that's good to hear. It's a sign of growing up."

She smiled, "But if you're ever looking for a girlfriend, I'm sure Fatima would be glad to fill the position." She nudged him, and laughed her quiet careful laugh.

That night, Oscar didn't get home until 2:00 am. Sebastian woke up when he heard the car door slamming and then Oscar fumbling with the key to the house. He got up and went down stairs in time to find his mother in her bath robe at the open door as Oscar stumbled in. He was more loud-mouthed than usual when drunk, and he stumbled in roaring greetings to his mother.

"*Shhh*, Oscarito, come now, let's go to bed."

Sebastian was disgusted, "Don't help him, mom, if he can't walk to his own bed, let him sleep on the floor."

"Sebastian, *shhh*, you'll wake your father."

"He might as well be woken up since I have!"

His mother shushed him, but ignored him as she put her arms around the mumbling Oscar and tried to help him up the stairs. "Maybe it would be best to postpone this trip for a few days." she whispered.

"A few days? You know as well as I do that it doesn't matter. There will always be a party to go to. You have got to stop babying him! He'll never grow up if you keep treating him this way – "

"Keep your voice down."

"I will not. This is shameful and disgusting! You have to teach him to hold his liquor or he'll have to join Alcoholics Anonymous."

They were at the top of the stair case, and she led her youngest son to his room across from Sebastian's room. "You're exaggerating. Any other night, and you would have been with him." she whispered and closed the bedroom door.

Sebastian shook his head, "You know I'm not *this* bad, Mama, I never have been. And besides, that's not the point! Any other night, I would be with him, but not tonight of all nights."

"Postpone the trip, Sebastian, I'll talk to your dad

about it."

"Mom, no. I'm going tomorrow, with or without Oscar!" he opened the door, walked into the hall, then turned, "Goodnight, mama." he said, and slammed his brother's bedroom door.

Chapter 4 – Darkness

The dawn was breaking over the mountains east of Acapulco, and the ocean was still dark, when Sebastian woke up.

The sky above Acapulco was beginning to turn gray as he knocked loudly on his brother's door, "Oscar," he said, his voice at a normal volume, "Get up. It's time to go."

His mother appeared in her doorway, "Sebastian – "she said.

"Get him up." he said to her, "Get a few extra clothes and stuff of his in a backpack. I'll wait in the car."

It was a striking figure that walked out of the house that morning. He walked quickly, and surely, his face sharply serious. He threw his own backpack in the backseat of the small, old car and looked at his watch.

In a few minutes, his mother came out with Oscar, who was walking to the car with his eyes closed. She led him to the car, seated him in the passenger seat, and put his backpack in the backseat. She wrapped her bathrobe around her and leaned into the driver's window and kissed Sebastian's cheek, "Take care of your brother." she said, "Be good, and call us."

"Yes mama, I will."

"I love you." she said.

He kissed her cheek then backed out of the driveway.

They drove through the beginnings of early morning traffic of Acapulco, but were soon released on to the open highway.

Oscar slept like a baby in the passenger seat. His face, under his messy hair and the hood of his sweatshirt, looked like the face of a little boy. His hair was always messy, but with his face lying expressionless, he looked completely childish and simple. It was the wild, playful face of his mother when he was awake, but asleep it was as though Sebastian was looking at his brother six years ago, when he was still a child. He looked like his mother, his face round and smooth, and his eyes big and a lighter tone of brown. Drusilla was the beauty of the family, but her appearance passed down to her son made him only cute, not handsome.

Sebastian, however, though his face was expressionless as well, as he looked ahead, had the opposite effect. He was like his father, who was oddly handsome. Odd, in that his features were sharp. Rarely did any of the smoothness of his mother appear in his face. His eyes were thin and jet black. His hair was neatly spiked with gel in the front, and his face was cleanly shaven coming to a point with his strong, yet strangely graceful chin. That gracefulness was the only trace of his mother. It wasn't the shape or expression of his face that was somehow like his mother, it was only a gentle whisper about the way he looked out on the world.

It was early June and the rainy season had started. It rained every day in the afternoon, but the mornings started crisp as the rain of the afternoon before cleaned the air. Sebastian drove the old family car easily and smoothly over the four-lane highway that at some points, stretched from mountain to mountain on bridges. He rolled down his window.

The wind became cool as he began to drive through the mountains outside the city. It was a damp morning and the air on the highway smelled like wet cement. He took a breath of the sandy, cool smell. It was a nice smell, and he vaguely smiled to himself. The love of these things was deeply hidden in him. Hidden, sometimes even from himself. It wasn't manly to be sentimental.

The early morning news broadcast from Mexico City came over the radio, and Sebastian listened intently. He had a sensible mind that craved knowledge. He was attentive, pondering politics, wars, recent events, and all the things the news anchor talked about.

When they got to Chilpancingo, the capital of Guerrero, they didn't stop. Their father would most definitely campaign in Chilpancingo. They weren't needed there. But Sebastian didn't forget to text his mother as they arrived there.

After the city of Chilpancingo, the road continued on, but turned into a two lane road through the mountains.

It was a little past noon when Oscar began to wake up. It took him a while to gain the will power to open his eyes to the bright sunlight. When he finally did, he squinted around him a moment and grinned at Sebastian, "Good morning," he whispered.

Sebastian grunted, and there was a long silence. Sebastian's many hours driving in the cool-smelling wind hadn't made him forget about the night before. "You got home late." he finally said.

"Huh?" Oscar yawned.

"You said the party would be over at twelve but you didn't come home until two. What were you doing those two hours?"

Oscar put his hand to his head, "Ah," he moaned, "A couple of us hung around a little longer."

"You got to be careful... These are dangerous, complicated times."

"Not now, Sebas, my head hurts. Besides, what does it matter? So, I stayed out a little longer, it's not like I'm getting hooked on drugs or something. What is it with you these days? You're so bossy... A few years ago, we were a team, but now you're always ordering me around." He closed his eyes and leaned his face on the window.

Sebastian didn't answer.

That afternoon they arrived in Tlapa de Commonfort. The highway seemed to have simply dropped them into the middle of the city. It was a large city in the middle of a mountainous desert, but though large, it had a very backward feel about it. It was as if hundreds of tiny towns had been piled together in the desert. The houses were cluttered together, and on top of each other. The streets were tiny, dusty and slithering among the houses as if the streets themselves were lost. The streets were crowded places and nearly all the people were Indian people. Most weren't dressed in native clothes, but you could tell they were Indian by their stern quiet faces.

There, they stopped at a gas station and saw a little old lady selling tacos to the people who came on buses and trucks from every direction. "Tacos! Tacos! Tacos!" she shouted. Sebastian didn't hesitate to get her attention.

They ate their tacos and drank their Coca-Colas under the hot sun as they leaned against the trunk of the car, but soon they were on their way.

Sebastian started driving, but after a few blocks in what he had thought was the right direction, he realized he didn't know how to get out of the city. He knew the direction they should be going in and he could see the mountains free from the city rising in that direction with the edges of city clinging to the bases, but the streets of the city were crisscrosses and dead ends.

They drove back and forth for over two hours until they started making their way in the right direction and realized the city was thinning out and the road they were on was leaving the city in the direction they wanted to be going. Soon the city released the road to the mountains, and they drove on the small two-lane road in the last of the afternoon sunshine.

As they gained altitude and distance, they left the desert and re-entered the crisp air and the pine trees. The clouds began building and soon it began to rain, and as it rained, the clouds bent down to touch the mountains. The rain and the fog, though light at first, became thicker.

There wasn't much traffic on the little road, only the occasional small Nissan pickup full of people coming from a village to Tlapa. However, as they drove slowly through the fog, a huge red truck with Coca-Cola written on the side, sped around the curve coming toward them. Sebastian swerved to the edge of the road as the truck went storming by, taking up both lanes as it sped past them.

"Did you see that?" Oscar gasped once it had passed.

"Of course, I saw that. We almost had a head-on collision."

"No, no, I mean the guys on the back with machine guns."

"Oh, yeah, the guards."

"Why do they have guards on the Coke truck?"

"Well, it's dangerous for them out in these places. It's a prime target for hold ups. Those trucks have quite a bit of money on them when they're coming back empty." He paused for a moment, "I've heard about stuff like that. I heard of one where there was a hold up and one of the men in the truck got killed. His widow was suing the Coke Company because her husband had worked for the company for half his life and they had five kids. I don't think the company gave her anything, though."

Oscar grunted.

"The company refused to compensate her because according to the driver of the truck - who survived - the man seemed to have recognized the killers, making it personal and not a casualty of his job. But everyone knows it wasn't really personal. The widow had a right to compensation, but the company just didn't want to pay her."

"How do you know all this?"

"My professor told us about it. His friend was the widow's lawyer."

Oscar was quiet for a while, "So that's the kind of place we're going to."

"Don't worry. We're not a Coke truck."

"Yeah, but such violent people. They could kidnap us for ransom when they find out we're the sons of a politician."

Sebastian laughed a quiet breathy laugh, "You're crazy. These people aren't that smart. They want cash at gun point and that's all. Besides, our dad isn't that well known yet. We're doing this to make him better known, remember?"

"Yeah, I guess." Oscar answered. "Where do they get their guns? I mean, they're illegal."

"Where do the drug traffickers get them? Where does anyone get them?" He shrugged, "How should I know? We don't study gun trafficking in law school."

"I hope we get there soon." Oscar said as they drove out of the fog and into the pure, hard rain.

It was only Oscar who seemed nervous, but as nightfall and the heavy rain swallowed up the remaining daylight, Sebastian was starting to get uncomfortable as well. The narrow road with sharp curves kept winding its way through the steep mountains. The air in the car felt thick and stuffy. And every curve seemed like it should be the last one before a town, but every curve only bent around to more pine trees. The car headlights barely dented the sea of darkness surrounding them, making the whole road a blur of grey.

They were moving at a steady speed when a noise came out of the darkness below them. Sebastian jumped. Oscar let out a yell. They could feel mud under the wheels as the car slowly came to a stop. Sebastian found that his legs were braced stiffly against the brake. He noticed now a total silence except for the rain pouring on the roof of the car. He couldn't see what was ahead because of the blanket of rain on the windshield. It was completely dark outside by now, and the headlights were just yellow balls of rain that were constantly changing with the movement of the water.

The silence was now just as deafening as the sound had been before, but they realized as the silence continued that they were sitting at a normal angle on seemingly flat ground.

They sat in silence. Nothing happened. Pulling the hood of his sweatshirt over his head and grabbing a small flashlight from his backpack, Sebastian got out of the car. He felt fresh watery mud slush up the sides of his Caterpillar boots with his first step. The rain hit him sharply. It penetrated his sweatshirt immediately and in a few moments his hood hung heavily around his face, the cloth full of rainwater. He couldn't see well, but he could tell that they were still on the road. He walked around to the front of the car, and in the light of the headlights he could see that they were in a stretch of about twenty feet where the pavement of the road had washed completely away. He could see that the pavement started again after that and though they were sitting in mud, it was relatively flat and could be driven on, so he got in the car again. The wheels spun and mud flew. The car seemed to hesitate, but soon they were on the pavement again.

Perhaps if Sebastian had known how many of these washouts there would be, he would have stopped right then, but he continued. Shortly afterward, though, they came to another washout like the last. The wheels spun through the mud and they came to the other side. They continued, and soon they found another and made it through. Every time they came to another washout they would make it through fully expecting it to be the last one and to see the lights of a town around the next bend in the road. But washout by washout, and the continuation of inky darkness made those expectations weaken.

Sebastian looked at the clock, it was nearly eleven, "Maybe we should go back," he said, but Oscar didn't answer.

He looked at Oscar. Through the darkness, he could only see dimly the outline of his profile, with the light of the radio and the reflection of the headlights. He looked ahead again. He had become able to distinguish a washout now, and he saw another one up ahead. He stopped a few feet from it. The rain was falling in sheets and the mud was losing its density.

"We could never make it back through all the washouts we've already come through, this rain is making them worse." Oscar pushed a button on his phone, the light of it nearly blinded him, but he squinted at it. There hadn't been a signal since Tlapa, but he couldn't help checking it to make sure. "And we might almost be there, or there might be fewer washouts up ahead." He mumbled hopeful words in a very unhopeful way, but at least the words themselves were hopeful.

With that spark of mumbled hope, Sebastian let out the clutch and the car rolled toward the mud ahead of them.

The wheels sunk as soon as they rolled off the pavement. They rolled a few more feet and then started spinning.

He kept his foot on the gas and the motor roared and the wheels spun like mad. He pushed in the clutch, let it out and tried again. He killed it. He cranked it and it started again.

"Oscar, get out and push."

"No way, I'll get my new white Converse all muddy!"

"Come on –"

"You're already wet and muddy, so you do it."

"Ok, whatever," Sebastian said and opened his door.

"Man, you gave in fast, you must really be tired!" Oscar exclaimed, but Sebastian slammed the door mid-sentence. "I guess he's not in the mood for jokes..." Oscar mumbled as he looked out at the shadow of his brother. He crawled across to the driver's seat and took the wheel in his hands.

Sebastian's boots wadded through the mud as he squinted through the rain. The rain glowed red in the taillights. He put his hands between the lights and pushed with all the strength in his tired muscles, but his hands only slid around on the wet metal. Oscar was pushing the gas and the wheels were throwing mud out behind them, but they weren't advancing.

He stopped trying to push and watched for a moment realizing that the wheels were digging themselves down deeper in the mud. They weren't getting out, they were sinking deeper.

He glanced around him. The lights of the car were

still the only lights in sight. They shone on dark trees, on the little rivers of brown water that flowed among the rocks and denser mud, and falling drops of rain. At a short distance, it made shapes on the pavement, in the ditch that became the side of the mountain, and in the trees on the other side where the mountain rose high above them.

Everything the light hit seemed distorted and ghostly. Sebastian's mind began to race, the ghost stories and superstitions of his childhood, the horror movies and murder shows, and the stories of the Indian people all became visible in what the dim light showed of the darkness. As his sense of logic was ripped from his mind and lost in the ghostly shadows, panic gripped him. He put his hands on the back of the car again and pushed with the strength that comes from fear.

In a second the motor stopped and with a sudden deathly silence the world went dark. The dark was so dense, it was as if someone had covered Sebastian's eyes and taken away his sight. He froze. Oscar had killed the motor. He could hear the rain and the water and could feel the car under his hands. Suddenly he felt his back was unguarded and he turned quickly with his back against the car. Just as he turned, he heard a sound and then the roar of the motor – and light! His sight was back, but so were the ghostly shapes. He swallowed and turned his back to the darkness again. He had to get them out of there.

Chapter 5 – Cochoapa El Grande

Sebastian opened his eyes and closed them again. Last night all he wanted was light, but now it was unbearable. He forced his eyes to open.

He was laying crookedly and half curled up in the front seat. His clothes had partly dried and were sticking to his skin. His back was stiff and he uncurled himself and stretched out. He turned and saw Oscar in the back seat. Oscar had in desperation also gotten out of the car the night before and this morning it showed with mud covering his Converse and making its way up his jeans, almost to his knees.

Sebastian blinked and saw past Oscar in the rear window what had woken him up. A big white truck was approaching them and wasn't twenty feet away.

He leaned over and shoved Oscar, "Wake up!" he said, then turned, opened the door and jumped out.

As the truck roared toward him he stood there, sleepy, damp, and muddy, with a stiff smile on his face.

The truck slowly and carefully dropped into the mud of the washed away road and pulled up next to the car. The motor roared loudly next to them, and Oscar shot up and began crawling out of the back seat.

Oscar was standing next to his brother a few seconds later, just as the driver of the truck walked around his truck and appeared in front of them. He was a white man, obviously a foreigner, with a graying blond beard and a balding head. He walked slowly, cautiously, yet somehow strongly. He walked like his truck drove.

"Good morning," he said, smiling with white teeth showing through his beard.

Sebastian stuck his hand out and the man shook it, but without saying anything more, the man leaned down and looked at the wheels. He said nothing, only nodded slightly and made his way to the back of his truck and began pulling out ropes and chains and began hooking them to the car. Sebastian quickly began helping him, and soon the man positioned his truck in front of the car. Sebastian got in the car and pushed the gas as the man pulled the car, but the car didn't struggle, it slid right out of the mud and rolled neatly on the pavement.

The man nodded and smiled again as he unhooked the car from his truck and began putting his things away.

The motor of the car was humming nicely. Oscar got

in the passenger seat and closed the door just as Sebastian let off on the clutch and pushed the gas. The motor roared but they didn't move forward.

"Something's wrong." he mumbled.

"Quit making jokes!" Oscar whined, his eyes red and abstract looking.

"No. Look." Sebastian let his foot off the clutch again and pushed the gas as Oscar watched.

The foreigner hadn't driven away yet, but having finished putting his things away he watched them for a moment. When they didn't drive away, he came to the car and leaned down to the driver's window, "Is something wrong?"

"Our car won't move," Oscar said in a tone of complaint.

In the warmth of the early morning sun, the foreigner leaned over the open hood of the car, and Sebastian looked under the car. Oscar sat slumped in the passenger seat looking down at his signal-less and dying phone.

It didn't take long for the foreigner's mechanical mind to figure out the trouble: a burnt-out clutch. He explained to them, absolutely absorbed in his explanation. Hearing the man speaking, Sebastian realized that the man spoke very clear and good Spanish.

When the man was done, Sebastian let his breath out and leaned against the car. During the explanation, Oscar had gotten out and was now leaning against the car next to his brother. "So what do we do, Oscar?" Sebastian mumbled.

"I could pull you to Cochoapa." the foreigner said, "Where were you going?"

"Metlatonoc. We have a job there."

"Well, Cochoapa isn't far from there and there's a good mechanic in Cochoapa. He could probably fix it. You could stay in Cochoapa where I stay."

Sebastian smiled in relief, "Thank you very much."

The man had to take everything out of his truck again and hook his truck to their car.

When they were hooked up, Sebastian let Oscar take the wheel of the car. He had an impulsive desire to ride in the truck with foreign man. He climbed into the passenger seat of the white truck and the man only smiled a small smile but said nothing.

The loud motor roared as the man drove slowly and carefully down the road. Sebastian leaned back comfortably in the big seat, noticing how roomy the inside of the truck was. For the first time that morning, Sebastian noticed how the sun was shining on the mountains and the air was crisp and clear.

"Where do you come from?" Sebastian asked him.

"Oaxaca" the man answered.

Sebastian was surprised, how could this man be from the neighboring state? The man must have noticed his confusion because he smiled, "I'm American, but I've lived in Oaxaca for over thirty years."

"Oh. Why did you come to Mexico?"

"My wife and I came here to teach people about the Bible."

"Oh." Sebastian said, and he suddenly didn't know how to respond. "The United States is a really nice place," he said, "Very organized – unlike Mexico." He laughed a little, "I have family in California, and my family has gone several times to visit."

The man smiled slightly, and nodded as if he heard but had nothing to say about it, and Sebastian suddenly wondered why he had told him all of that.

They drifted into silence. In a few minutes they came upon a washout in the road. Sebastian felt the color drain from his face. Half the road was gone into a landslide down the side of the mountain. "If we had gotten here last night –" He blurted out.

The man nodded, "You could have fallen off the mountain." His ears turned red and he pulled a small lever for the four-wheel drive. He began to drive, really near to the mountain wall, but still Sebastian's heart pounded as he looked down at how near the wheel was to the edge. "You have to get out and guide your brother."

Sebastian looked up in surprise. But, of course.

It was a relief to be out of the truck, but a terror to watch it crawl over the rocks near the edge where the road once had been.

When he finally got back in and they continued on their way, he couldn't help wonder how close they could have come to driving over that edge the night before.

In only about an hour, Sebastian saw a small town lying on a long ridge across the valley.

"That's Cochoapa El Grande." the American said.

After a few more curves, they lost sight of it and began to slowly descend between the mountains. They got to a point where the land wasn't really flat, but to the left of the road there was a town, slightly bigger than Cochoapa, cradled between the mountains.

"This is Metlatonoc."

Sebastian craned his neck as the man turned on the road to the right.

They drove along the cradle of the two ridges next to a creek. The mountains were green and the water in the creek was muddy brown. It was a strange sensation, but around every curve Sebastian was expecting to see something, to understand how they were going to get to the tiny town on the ridge. He was waiting for something, yet just as his mind began to wonder, they went around the final curve.

The town spread on the hill before him and surprised Sebastian. The hill it was on didn't look like the majestic pointed ridge he had seen from a distance. The town before him lay on a rounded hill under an even taller mountain that stood shining blue in the noon sunshine.

The town itself was dominantly brown. The roofs, though standing in the sunshine, did not shine because they were made of dull tar paper hammered on with nails through metal bottle caps. Among these, a few roofs of tin shined in the sun, but the whole of the picture was dull and ugly.

Up, between the houses, there was a line of reddish dirt, but the only colors of the town that could be seen from this distance were the dark brown roofs, red dirt and an occasional shining tin roof or a lonely tree top. What he had first seen on the ridge was majestic, but what he saw now was a dirty little town smeared across a pretty mountain.

They drove into a little dip where one mountain turned into another and the town went out of site. They crossed a little bridge over the same winding muddy creek, and followed the road as it stretched up the side of the new hill. At the top of the hill, there was a big cement archway that was painted yellow and had written on it in red paint, 'Bienvenido a Cochoapa El Grande', and in one more curve after that, the town was once again before them, now larger. It took only one more dip and another tiny bridge and they were in the town.

Almost immediately the American pulled a little off the road and stopped his truck. "Here to the right is the mechanic shop."

They unhooked their car in front of a shabby board house that had a sign on it that said, '*Se Vende Gasolina*'. A short man wandered outside and nodded distantly as the American explained to him. The man wore an old faded t-shirt and looked at them with dull, sleepy eyes. He nodded blankly again and mumbled in a deep, accented and sandy voice that he would have to get the parts from Tlapa, but that it would only take a few days. Sebastian's heart sank, but what more could he expect? He and Oscar reluctantly got their backpacks out of the back seat, and out of the trunk they got the rolls of their father's campaign posters, as well as the large canvas with his picture and name on it.

The American was obviously a man of few words, and when they took their things out of their car, not a word was said. They put their things in the white truck, and Sebastian didn't speak until the American sat down in the drivers' seat. He opened his mouth to apologize to him and ask him where there would be a place to stay, but before he could, the American said, "You can stay at the church. I'm sure no one will mind. It's just a few blocks away. You can come and check on your car whenever you want."

"Thank you." Sebastian said, a little surprised. "What is your name, sir?"

"Samuel Clarmont," the American smiled.

"Nice to meet you, I'm Sebastian Miguel Arroyo Espinoza, and this is my brother Oscar Bernardino Arroyo Espinoza,"

"Nice to meet you." Oscar mumbled.

Samuel smiled.

They drove very slowly down the muddy street. Children who had been playing in the street stopped for a moment to stare and then they ran along the side of the truck yelling at the top of their lungs in Mixteco. Sebastian looked down from the truck bewildered at them. They were very small, thin children with shabby and muddy clothes. Their skin was not really darker than his own, but it was dry and seemed to have a layer of fine, dry mud on it.

Sebastian looked up from the children and found their older siblings, and parents standing outside their houses. There were old women, their faces covered in wrinkles, their hair grey and thin, hanging like long strings from their scalp. There were middle aged women, at least they appeared to be middle aged, most of which carried a young child. When they looked up, however, Sabastian saw in their faces that they were really very young. Then there were very young women, nearly girls who looked up at the men in the truck and smiled slightly. Most of the woman were dressed in the colorful woven *huipiles* and full neon colored skirts. Many of the girls wore blue jeans but the bottom of their jeans were edged with red mud and their shoes and shirts were distinctly Indian.

His eyes found the faces of the men, old and young, that they too, appeared much older, most of them leaned by their doorways, sleepily looking out over the street. A few young men in white tank tops with rounded muscular arms glowing, carried picks and shovels and walked down the street.

Sebastian only watched them, he had no time to react or think about it because soon the white truck pulled down a narrow street and with difficulty, started to back the long truck into a little kind of driveway between three small structures. The one to the right was a simple board building, and when Samuel began to back up, a man came out of the open door. Sebastian barely got a glance at the man, but he knew he wasn't from there.

The building behind them, was a long white building made out of some sort of white tin, with brown wooden doors facing the outside. The building to their left was really the skeleton of a building with a cement floor, a tin roof and support beams holding the roof up, but with no walls.

They came to a stop with the back of the truck only a few feet from the white building. The man came to the driver's window, "Samuel!" he said, "Welcome!" He had a distinctly bold voice, and very serious eyes that looked into the back seat. "You have brought us guests."

Sebastian and Oscar got out of the truck and were met by the man's warm handshake. "Welcome to your home." he said, politely, "My name is Gregorio." As he spoke, a woman and a teenage boy appeared out of the white house. Turning to them he said, "This is my wife, Vero, and my son Gabriel." Sebastian and Oscar shook their hands and mumbled their full names.

Gregorio had a round, handsome face, and comical ears. Something about him was very serious, however, he only slightly, yet not insincerely, smiled at his guests. His wife, Vero, however, had a long face with a long, pointed nose and her smile never left her face. Their son was an odd mixture of both. He seemed to have gotten the handsomeness of his father as well as the funny ears, yet he also had the long nose and the ever-present smile of his mother. They had obviously been a very typical Mexican city-family. They reminded Sebastian of many of his own family members and friends. Gregorio and Vero had the distinct air of educated Mexicans, but as to their son, Sebastian couldn't understand him immediately. He was like his parents, yet he was not. His air was something Sebastian had never known before.

It was nearing the afternoon when they arrived. They stood awkwardly around the white truck as Samuel talked to Gregorio about things they knew nothing about, until Vero came to them and said, "Get your things and come with me." They followed her the few feet to the white tin house. She opened one of the wooden doors and they followed her inside. It was a very small room with a clean cement floor, held up by wooden beams, containing two twin size beds and a shabby bedside table. "I only made one of the beds, but I'll put sheets on the other one before tonight. You guys make yourself comfortable and put your things down. The men forget basic hospitality, but don't worry, you guys are welcome. If you need anything else, I will be in the kitchen two doors, that way," she pointed a long finger to her right, "And the outhouse is around the corner that way," she pointed to the left, "You can't miss it."

"Thank you very much." Sebastian said finally, "I'm very sorry to impose on you this way –"

"No imposition at all!" Vero interrupted with a smile, and like a wind she went out the door, but then she opened it up again, "Oh, I'm making food. It'll be ready in a few minutes. When you're ready just come to the kitchen. That way." She pointed a finger again and disappeared.

When she was gone, Sebastian sat down on the edge of the bed and sighed. His clothes were dried against his skin and he suddenly realized how tired he was.

"Well this is awkward." Oscar said. He was standing near the door with his hands in his pockets with his backpack next to his feet.

Sebastian looked at his brother for a moment, then he said half yawning, "You look terrible."

The rest of the day passed very slowly for Sebastian. They ate with the family and with Samuel. Samuel told them all about the burnt-out clutch, and they talked more about things Sebastian didn't know or didn't pay any attention to. Vero talked to them. She asked them all about themselves and smiled in at them through their fuzzy sleepiness.

After they ate, Sebastian noticed that the sun was dipping lazily behind the mountains. It seemed as if it took hours to move in the sky, but as soon as the light began to disappear, he thanked them all again and excused himself and his brother.

"Are you sure," Vero said, "Wouldn't you like to take a bath?"

Sebastian paused for a moment and thought of the clothes that clung to him, "That actually sounds really good." he had to admit.

Vero smiled, "Gabriel, go start the fire."

That evening, in a little wooden stall next to the outhouse, Sebastian took his first bucket bath with hot water that had been heated over an outdoor fire. As he let a dipper full of warm water run down his face, he thought for a moment that in the water he smelt the smell of burning pine as if the smell had gotten into the water particles themselves.

He thought he would be asleep the moment his head hit the pillow, but he laid there for a moment, his eyes wide open in the dark. He could hear the family, Samuel, and a television in one of the adjoining rooms. It was a somewhat pleasant sound. He closed his eyes and put his arm across his nose and took a deep breath. Yes. His skin, under the smell of cheap bar soap, had a faint smell of burning pine.

Chapter 6 – Music in the Wind

The morning sun rose over the crisp, blue-green mountains of the rainy season and it shone on a wet and muddy pair of Caterpillar boots and a pair of All Star sneakers. The sun rose higher in the blue sky, drying the earth and the shoes.

The light knocked on Sebastian's eyelids until he opened them, and when he did, he jumped up, realizing first that he didn't hear the ocean. In an instant, he remembered where he was and grabbed his wrist-watch from the night stand—8:07, it read. He lay back down for a moment. It surprised him, but he felt comfortable. He lay there listening for a moment and he heard music playing and pots rattling. He sighed and rolled out of bed.

In the twin bed next to Sebastian, Oscar's face was lost in the pillow and under the blankets but his arms were spread out and dangling on either side of the bed. Sebastian grinned and pushed his brother. The bed jiggled like Jell-O and Oscar, without opening his eyes, pushed his brother back and stuffed his face into the pillow.

When Sebastian walked into the kitchen, Vero was alone setting the table. She looked up at him and smiled, "Did you sleep well?"

"Yes, thank you." Sebastian smiled slightly in return, "Can I help you with something?"

She looked surprised for a moment, "Oh, well, ok. You can finish putting these around." She set down her handful of silverware and moved over to the stove. Sebastian began putting the silverware neatly next to each plate.

"So, what's your family like?" she asked. "Samuel told us that your dad is the politician Draco Arroyo. Pardon my ignorance, but I've actually never heard of him."

Sebastian sighed a laugh that sounded more like a grunt. "He's not that well known."

"And your mom? What's she like?"

"She's..." Sebastian could feel Vero looking at him, "She's very pretty and nice."

He sensed Vero's smile as she turned back to her work. "That's so sweet. I love to hear sons say things like that about their mothers. I've never heard Gabriel say stuff like that about me, but I guess he'd never say it in front of me."

Sebastian didn't know what to say, so he didn't say anything.

Vero, however, only paused and continued, "I worry sometimes about Gabriel. He's lived here since he was very young, but he's not quite like the people here. I guess all mothers worry about their kid's future. But, yet, God put him here so He knows why and what will come of him. I never thought I would live here, either, and much less for all this time."

"How long?" Sebastian ventured.

She turned and smiled, "Ten years."

"That's a lot of time." he paused. He wanted to ask why, yet, he didn't want to ask why. They ran a church; the answer would be obvious. "Where are you from?"

"Mexico D.F." she answered. "Well, I went there to study, at least. I'm originally from a little town in Veracruz. I went all big and grand to study and became a lawyer."

"Lawyer?"

"Yup, but well, God had other plans. I mean, I did get my degree, but I never actually started practicing." She laughed to herself, "I met Gregorio. I thought he went to that university to study something important, he sure acted like it, but turns out he was an out-of-work art student. He was crazy in those days. His clothes where always paint-stained and his hair was never neat, but boy, he sure held his head high. If being an artist wasn't crazy enough, he went around with this group of kids that were always preaching on street corners. 'The evangelists', we called them. Ok, well, they weren't always exactly preaching, but, they sure stood out in the crowds. They were different and they weren't shy about it. I kind of liked them. I started trying to hang around in that crowd, but, I guess you could say they were exclusive, you were welcome but you never could really stay unless you became like them. Boy, they started preaching at me. At least that's what if felt like, until, well, until what they said actually made sense. It was that crazy artist boy that actually helped me most though, and with his help, I became a Christian."

Sebastian watched her as she grinned at the skillet in front of her. "That was the beginning," she said, "But true to reality, we had a lot to go through after that, both individually and as a couple. He quit school and started to work." she laughed quietly again, he had to get a 'real' job, he never actually became that grand artist. When I finished school, I married him. And well, right around when Gabriel was born he decided to go to Bible school and mission's school and one thing led to another, and here we are." she looked up at Sebastian and smiled.

He didn't know how to answer, but before he had time to think about it, Gregorio came into the kitchen, and nodded his head solemnly at Sebastian. Sebastian couldn't help but smile slightly at him. He looked nothing like who Vero had described. Vero glanced at

Sebastian and then burst into laughter. Gregorio looked confused for only a moment and then only nodded, "Vero's been telling you about me."

"Oh, Gregorio!" Vero sighed when she finished laughing.

Soon Oscar, Samuel, and Gabriel joined them in the kitchen. There was silence among most of them. Vero talked a lot and Sebastian found himself the one who was most expected to answer. Somehow that comfort he had felt that morning when he woke up, hadn't really left him.

Their cell phones hadn't had signal since the day before last, and Sebastian knew his mother would be worried, so after breakfast they asked for directions to the nearest place that had a phone. It turned out that there was only one *caseta* in that town.

The sun was warm on their skin as they began to walk down the dirt street. It was peaceful, though they weren't alone. That morning they became aware of that there seemed to always be a small crowd of children hanging around the house where Vero and Gregorio lived. Sometimes they were running and shouting, playing their games, and sometimes they were just watching them.

They tried to ignore the little group of kids following them, staring at them and talking to each other in their language. The fact they were there made Sebastian too uncomfortable to talk to his brother, yet, he realized that even if they weren't there he wouldn't have said anything to his brother, and he wouldn't have cared either way. Suddenly, having eyes on him all the time made him very conscious of everything he was doing and not doing.

The caseta was a tiny wooden house like all the others, except it had a dusty printed tarp with a white woman's face on it. Through the dust and wrinkles of the tarp, you could tell the woman was supposed to be an operator.

Sebastian ducked through the small doorway into a dark little room with Oscar following close behind him. It was a very empty and dark room. There was one woman sitting on a woven *petate* among a few scattered pieces of cloth, and a young girl who stood up from a little wooden chair when they walked in. She led them to a little wooden booth. They gave her the number and then they both squeezed into the little booth and closed the door half way. Inside on a little shelf was an off-white telephone. Sebastian held the receiver and listened to it ring.

"Hello?" his mother's voice sounded distant.

"Hi, Mama."

"Sebas? Thank goodness! I've been worried sick. How are you? How's Oscar? Are you ok? Did something happen?"

"We're fine. It's just the car. We're calling from a caseta in a town called Cochoapa El Grande. We'll probably be out of here in a few days. They have to send for the parts in Tlapa."

"Oh, ok." she paused a moment, then her tone changed a little and she began in her chipper, not really serious, voice, "You need to come home soon. There are so many things going on here that you will be missing out on if you stay there much longer. Fatima's family is giving her that party for graduation you know, I just got the invitation today. I heard her mother say that they're having it later so everyone can be there. I know that means they want you to be there. Oh, Fatima called yesterday because she was worried because you hadn't answered her texts. I didn't know you guys texted each other." She giggled slightly, "I know she'll be relieved to know you're ok."

"This phone call is costing a lot of money, I think." Sebastian said.

"Oh, right. Sorry." her voice lost its playfulness, "How are you and Oscar getting along?"

Sebastian hadn't expected that question, "Fine, I guess." he said.

"Oh good. I thought maybe this little trip together would do you both a lot of good."

"Yeah."

"Let me talk to him."

Sebastian handed the phone to his brother, who was leaning awkwardly against the wall of the booth.

Sebastian leaned uncomfortably for a few minutes until Oscar handed him the phone again, "It's dad," he said.

"Son?" his father's voice burst from the telephone wires as soon as Sebastian put the phone to his ear. "Where are you staying son?"

"It's a little town called Cochoapa el Grande."

"I know, I know, your mom wrote the name down. Where in the town are you staying?"

"Oh, a missionary is letting us stay at a church here."

"A missionary?" Draco's voice didn't get louder, it merely got dryer as he repeated the words slowly. "Is the missionary foreign?"

"One is American, the others are from Mexico City."

"Christians, Mormons, what are they?"

"Christians, I think."

Draco was silent for only an instant, then his voice came through clearly and slowly. "Be careful, son. Don't you get brainwashed."

"Ok, but they're really friendly, I don't think we need to worry..."

"And the campaign? How much have you done, have you started? We have more than just that region to do, you know."

"Well, we haven't really started."

"Start." Draco said simply.

"Well, we can't do much but just give the posters and stuff to the local office."

"You haven't done even that yet?" Again, his voice

sounded dry, "Do it. Today. And not just that, if you'll be hanging around, hang posters, talk to the leaders, and do stuff. You aren't just errand-boys, you're my sons, and you need to be active. You need to represent me well; you never know when you will have to represent yourself in the same way. This isn't just for your father's political career, but it means a lot for your futures as well. Don't play around, this is very serious and important for all of our futures. You don't know how much of our futures depend on the choices made in those little towns full of little, un-important people."

"Yes, I understand. I will do my best, although I'm not sure I know how to represent you publicly."

"You represent me every day of your life, son." he paused, "Besides, you're going to be a lawyer, aren't you? You need to learn these things."

"I know. But it's different here. I don't know how to make Indian people understand politics."

Draco laughed slightly in little puffs coming from his

nose, "No, no, you don't make them understand, you use their ignorance. Their minds are pliable, and ignorant. You don't create independent thought – you just tell them what they should think."

Sebastian was silent.

"Listen to me, son." his father's voice said.

Sebastian didn't know what to say, a quiet anger was stirring in him, though he didn't really know why. "Ok dad." he said finally.

There wasn't much to say after that, and after a short goodbye from his mother to him and Oscar, he hung up the phone, left the booth, and paid the young girl who again got up from her wooden chair.

As they walked back up the street with the small crowd of staring children, Sebastian felt that small burning anger. He didn't try to figure it out, he only felt it. That caused a determination in his walk. He turned to Oscar half way home and told him, through clenched jaws, "We're going to that other town. We're going to talk to the authorities."

They came back to the house and got their rolls of posters and their giant canvas. When they were leaving again, Vero saw them and smiled, "Where are you going? Did you talk to your parents?"

"Yes. We're going to Metlatonoc." Sebastian mumbled, his mouth in a straight line.

His anger was unconsidered by himself, it took the form of determination in his mind. It was a form of power, an acting power that was the source of Sebastian's hard work. In the last few days it had mellowed, but listening to his father had brought it back to him. As he walked down the long road in the middle of town, it did not mellow, it stayed strong despite the slow walk and the people watching him as he passed. When they arrived by the main road and he heard a small truck coming up the road from behind them, Sebastian didn't look, he just waved him arm and glanced in that direction. The truck stopped and they swung themselves in the back. They rode to Metlatonoc on the bumpy road with their heads held high.

The truck stopped for them in front of the *presidencia* of Metlatonoc. They jumped out of the back and paid the driver. Sebastian glanced up at the building for a moment, but successfully covered up his impression. It was a huge, square, yellow building with a long porch and grand stairs leading to the porch.

He straightened his spine and with Oscar next to him he walked up the stairs.

There was a group of men sitting on benches and chairs on the porch. Sebastian kept his walk steady, he wasn't sure who they were, but they must be the town officials. When he got near them he could smell beer, and he saw bottles on the ground. A few looked up at him, swaying with their eyes cloudy. For a moment he hesitated, then moved toward the most sober looking man.

"Good day, sir," Sebastian said, extending his hand but keeping his expression formal. "I'm here as a representative of the pre-candidate of our party, Draco Arroyo."

The most sober man stood to his feet and nodded, mumbling and leading them to a metal door facing the big porch. He led them inside, and told them to please have a seat and he would gather the rest of the town officials.

The man left. Oscar sat down in one of the old wooden chairs, while Sebastian walked around the room. It was a big room, but half empty. There was one wooden table and a dozen scattered chairs. On the walls, there were a few dusty and fading posters of old candidates.

In a few minutes, the man came back with most of the men who were on the porch. It had taken him a while to convince a few of them to come in, and when they did, they came in staggering and glassy-eyed. Most of the men found a chair and sat and said very little, but there was one man who came in, and staggered toward Sebastian. "Good day, good day." he slurred, "We are a poor people." He straightened himself and took Sebastian's hand, "We need the government's help. Our women need money and the kids need food. We are a poor people."

Sebastian pulled his hand from the man's grasp, "Yes, take a seat please."

"I, I, am a good man. I work hard," the man waved his hand through the air, "I work."

"Yes – "

"Stupid government. Oh, but not you! We will win, we will live better!"

A more sober man led the man away from Sebastian, but now Sebastian was confused and didn't know what to say. He tried to speak boldly about his father's plans and policies as if they were his own. He tried to explain it all as he understood it, but the drunk men's glassy-eyes and loud shouts of incompetent agreement only disturbed and interrupted Sebastian. In a few moments, he gave up and asked if they could hang the poster of Draco Arroyo on the front of the building. All the men nodded but nobody moved.

"If it could be done right now..." Sebastian said.

Finally, the sober man went out and called a few young boys who brought rope. Under Sebastian's close supervision, they climbed up to the roof of the *presidencia,* and dropped the canvas with Draco Arroyo's face and slogan down the front of the building.

They left the sober man in charge of the rolls of posters they brought, and after shaking all the men's hands, and pulling away from the loud one, they made their way down the steps of the building.

At the bottom of the steps they stopped and looked up at the giant canvas again.

"It's impressive." Oscar said.

Sebastian glanced at him, he'd been very quiet since

they had gotten here. He looked back up at the canvas, it really was impressive. His father's sharp eyes so familiar, but the half smile that he wore in the picture was so rare. It was impressive, but somehow, as they turned and walked down the street toward the main road again, Sebastian became aware of an impression that the canvas had given him. He thought of it in silence in the back of a pickup truck, and as they walked back up the streets of Cochoapa El Grande, and when they arrived, he knew what the impression was. It was all a lie, and with that thought it wasn't only an impression, it was the truth. The half-smile, the phone call, and the man Sebastian pretended to be in front of the town officials, was all a lie.

This thought made Sebastian feel suddenly very tired. He didn't want to talk, he didn't want to think.

When they ate their lunch with the people of the house, Sebastian hardly felt like listening to Vero telling him about homeschooling her son. He listened, he nodded, but he didn't care.

After lunch, all he wanted was to go shut himself in the room and pretend he was away from this place, away from his family, in some classroom with his classmates, on the beach with his friends, somewhere where he wasn't left with his thoughts. But after lunch they all began to set up chairs under the pavilion-building, and Vero asked for his help. He couldn't refuse, it was the least he could do because these people were giving them a place to stay and food to eat.

Only when Gabriel sat down up front and began strumming a guitar did Sebastian realize what was going to happen. He turned around, hoping to leave before he was invited to stay, but he found himself with Indian people coming in and sitting down.

He searched the room for Oscar and he found him a few yards away signaling panic to him with his eyes, just as Sebastian was going to try to make his way out, Vero appeared between them with two books in her

116

hand, "Come, Sebastian, Oscar, have a seat anywhere."
She smiled and handed them each a book.

Sebastian sighed, "Thank you." he said, and as she
left, he shrugged at Oscar.

He knew all eyes were on them, so he pulled Oscar
to the nearest seats and sat down. As he sat down, he
became aware that the girl he had sat down next to was
looking at him with large brown eyes. He looked at her
and said, "Good Afternoon," trying not to sound too
irritated.

The girl nodded and quickly looked away.

The people stood up and started to sing along with
Gabriel. They began to clap. Sebastian stood up but left
his hands in his pockets. The music came from the
guitar, but the people's singing ruined it. They were off-
key, and their clapping was all in the wrong time.
Sebastian looked at Oscar, who was still sitting, Oscar
looked up at him like a miserable puppy.

It was a relief when the music was over with, but

Sebastian knew what was coming next. He looked down at the book in his hands, and of course, it was a Bible. He sat down with a slump and felt the girl's eyes on him again.

When Samuel walked up to the front, he straightened up again. For some reason, he had expected Gregorio to talk, not Samuel, and something about Samuel interested him.

Samuel stood up in front and set his Bible on the pulpit. An Indian girl stood next to him and began to translate everything he said, "Good afternoon, let's read Ecclesiastes 1:8-11." he said.

Sebastian looked down blankly at the paper-back Bible in his hands. He felt the girl looking at him again. He wished she would stop looking at him. In the middle of his wish she reached for the Bible in his hand, he saw her small dark hands taking it from his hands and he looked up at her. She smiled a small rose-like smile with her rosy lips, and began flipping the pages of the paper back.

Her hands moved skillfully through the pages as he watched her. She didn't look like the other girls. Her hair was a nest of long curls, and her skin was sandy and darker than most of those in the town, those of which had a yellow hew in their skin. She was dressed like most of the other young girls, with a short huipil and a smooth skirt. Her lavender skirt contrasted with the yellow ribbons of her huipil, but the yellow dominated and it seemed to shine on her sandy skin like sunshine. Suddenly she was looking at him, and he was startled. She was holding the paperback Bible and pointing at something on the page, then he understood. He took the Bible and unintentionally smiled at her.

"'All things are full of labor; man cannot express it.'" Samuel said, and Sebastian looked down at the page where the girl pointed.

Oscar grunted and leaned over to see the Bible in Sebastian's hands.

"The eye is not satisfied with seeing nor the ear filled with hearing. That which has been is what will be, that which is done is what will be done, and there is nothing new under the sun. Is there anything of which it may be said, 'See, this is new'? It has already been in ancient times before us. There is no remembrance of former things, nor will there be any remembrance of things that are to come by those who will come after."

Oscar grunted again, "How depressing," he mumbled.

Sebastian was surprised that Oscar was paying attention. Sebastian didn't feel like listening, he preferred to watch the girl next to him – he found her much more interesting than what Samuel was reading – but since Oscar was listening, Sebastian leaned forward a little to listen to what Samuel was going to say about what he had just read.

"From this we can draw the conclusion found in Chapter 11 verse 9,"

The girl leaned over and turned a few pages of the Bible and pointed again.

"Rejoice, O young man, in your youth, and let your heart cheer you in the days of your youth; walk in the ways of your heart, and in the sight of your eyes..."

Oscar grinned oddly, "I like that part," he mumbled.

"But," Samuel looked up, almost as if he had heard Oscar, *"But know that for all these God will bring you into judgment."*

An old lady agreed loudly in Mixteco when the girl next to Samuel finished her translation. Something made Sebastian forget about the girl and his brother. Was it the word judgment? He remembered for a moment the warning of his father, it was something about brainwashing, but he wasn't sure. He just listened as Samuel said something else and the girl flipped through the pages for him again. He read along as Samuel read, *"For the wrath of God is revealed from heaven against all ungodliness and unrighteousness of men, who suppress the truth in unrighteousness."*

Judgment. Wrath. Oscar was right, it was depressing. Why not ignore it? It's only true if you believe it. But, if it was true, wasn't it true for everyone? Not believing it won't make it go away. He began to listen to Samuel, almost eagerly.

Samuel began reading from another place, *"But He was wounded for our transgressions, He was bruised for our iniquities; the chastisement for our peace was upon Him, and by His stripes we are healed. All we like sheep have gone astray; we have turned, everyone, to his own way; and the LORD has laid on Him the iniquity of us all."*

Samuel began to explain how what he had just read had been a prophecy about Jesus. Jesus. Of course. Where did he come into the depressing things Samuel had read? Sebastian knew very little about Jesus, what he knew was the wax figures in the Catholic Church. He remembered when he was little, he would go walking with his mother in *La Catedral* in the *zocalo* of Acapulco. He remembered walking all around the edges where there were the statues and framed pictures of Jesus and Mary and all the different saints. He only recalled seeing Jesus dead. But the way Samuel said the name, it sounded different than how Sebastian had heard it. He wasn't talking about a dead guy, or a wax figure, but he wasn't saying the name as if it was a guy down the street named Jesus, either. He spoke with reverence not given to man nor image.

The way he spoke, it frightened Sebastian. All the words Samuel said about Jesus seemed to make sense, and it was frightening.

"Ho! Everyone who thirsts, come to the waters; and all you who have no money, come, buy and eat. Yes, come, buy wine and milk without money without price. Why do you spend money for what is not bread, and your wages for what does not satisfy? Listen carefully to Me, and eat what is good, and let your soul delight itself

in abundance. Incline your ear, and come to Me. Hear, and your soul shall live; and I will make an everlasting covenant with you – the sure mercies of David." Samuel read and Sebastian listened, but he didn't understand.

He looked at Oscar, and was surprised to see Oscar nodding slowly. He looked at Sebastian and his eyes didn't look unfeelingly drab, but they sparkled a little, but not with joy, but with a terrible sadness. When he saw this, it frightened him even more. Did Oscar understand what he didn't?

The sun was beginning to set and the evening wind began to blow in the pine trees, releasing their aroma. The girl turned the pages of the Bible again and Sebastian's eyes fell on the page. *"If we confess our sins, He is faithful and just to forgive our sins and to cleanse us from all unrighteousness."*

"Amen," Samuel said, with no explanation, as if that one sentence solved everything. Gabriel started strumming on his guitar again, and the people bowed their heads and began to pray out loud, mostly in the Indian language. They made so much noise. Sebastian couldn't think. He looked over at his brother who was staring down at the floor, his eyes glassy. Sebastian bowed his head just in case someone was watching him. He looked down and saw the Bible in his hands. He began thumbing through the pages, *"Let the lying lips be put to silence."* That didn't make him feel better. He turned the pages, *"He considers all their works."* Why did these words make him so uncomfortable? They were just words. Nothing more, yet, nothing less.

Nothing less...

His skin was sensitive to the wind touching it and weaving its way through his stiff black hair. The music became clearer and Sebastian became aware of a pain in the pit of his stomach. He looked down at the Bible again and found a page between the two he had just read and found a column, *"When I kept silent, my bones grew old through my groaning all day long. For day and night Your hand was heavy upon me; my vitality was turned into the drought of summer. I acknowledged my sin to You, and my iniquity I have not hidden, I said, 'I will confess my transgressions to the LORD,' and You forgave the iniquity of my sin. For this cause, everyone who is godly shall pray to You in a time when You may be found..."*

He looked at the muddy cement floor for a long time, his mind shouting out how annoyed it was, but his heart seemed bent over in undefinable pain. He wanted to get out of there, but he was afraid now to be alone with himself... He realized as he stared at the ground what he had been feeling for a very long time. He didn't know how long it was since he liked himself. He disliked himself, now more than ever.

Gabriel's clear singing voice rose up above all the noises that annoyed Sebastian so badly. "Propitious are you, Lord, for me," he heard the boy singing, "Strong tower, refuge, my hope is centered in you. I always trust you, you are my strength. You are my strong refuge

God, because of your love, I'm more than a conqueror.

Today my life is complete in you."

Chapter 7 – Real

The music faded, and not too soon for Sebastian.

The people stood up and sang one last song. Sebastian

didn't clap, but he saw that Oscar was. This irritated

him, but when that music stopped and the people began

moving around, Oscar left his side without a word and

began to talk to Samuel. He couldn't hear them; he

didn't want to hear them.

He turned and started walking towards the back of

the building, wanting nothing but to escape to the room

where he could face himself alone.

Gregorio was suddenly in front of Sebastian,

"Rosalía!" he exclaimed, "How are you?"

Sebastian realized he wasn't talking to him, but he

couldn't get past him.

"I'm fine. Everything is normal." The girl who had been sitting next to him answered Gregorio in a very quiet voice. He had forgotten about her.

"That's good." Gregorio said, but his voice and expression were so serious it gave Sebastian the impression that this wasn't a casual conversation.

Sebastian put on a small smile and was about to say excuse me and slip past, when Vero appeared from somewhere behind him, "Gregorio!" she said, "What's wrong with you?"

"What did I do?" Gregorio said, his expression over-concerned.

"What did you do? What didn't you do? You're supposed to introduce our guest."

"Why of course. Rosalía, this is Sebastian. Sebastian – Rosalía."

They exchanged handshakes, but Sebastian didn't want to look the girl in the face. Somehow, he felt that if she saw his face, she would see all the things he hated about himself.

"Are you staying for dinner, Rosalía?" Gregorio asked her.

She looked around. The light was quickly disappearing. She nodded.

The lights had gone out that night, and there were a few short candles lined up on the kitchen table. Everyone was quiet, concentrating on trying to see their food.

Oscar had sat next to Samuel, leaving Sebastian next to Gregorio and across from Rosalía. He was glad no one could see his face clearly, and he was glad that there were other people who seemed to not want to talk either. Throughout dinner, no one said anything to him, and for that he was grateful, but he noticed the girl kept looking up at him with round eyes that shone in the candle light. They were heartbreaking eyes. They seemed to see deeper into him than Sebastian himself could see.

Sebastian hadn't noticed before, but the people at the other end of the table were talking about politics. The conversation was led by Oscar who was confirming how the PRD and most other political parties were corrupt. Sebastian was shocked as he watched Oscar nodding his head with what looked like an overwhelming sense of justice. Sebastian's face grew red with anger, and he was once again grateful for the candle light. He told himself that he was angry for the sake of his family's reputation, but he knew that in his anger, there was no sense of justice, and that made him all the more angry, realizing it was his brother's sudden sense of justice that filled him with jealousy.

"You know," Gregorio suddenly said, "I never really thought of it, but going to all these places to campaign must be hard work." He glanced at Sebastian, "Isn't it Sebastian?"

"Yes." Sebastian said bluntly, looking down at his food, ignoring all the eyes that watched him.

"Will you be needing help?"

Sebastian sighed loudly, "Yes, well, normally the people are supposed to do most of it."

"Well, we should get you some help. Gabriel could help you in the afternoons when he's done with his homework." Gabriel looked up, grinned and wiggled his eyebrows at Sebastian. Sebastian stared at him glumly, extremely irritated at the boy's goofiness. "Let's see, who else?" Gregorio stroked his chin in a way that looked far too dramatic. That irritated Sebastian as well, "Rosalía, how about your cousin?"

The girl hesitated, "Manuel?" she almost whispered the name.

"Yes! That would be perfect." Gabriel went back to his food, "Tell him, that he has a job – that it's his turn to help his government." He grinned a little and Gabriel laughed.

It wasn't funny to Sebastian, and he didn't care.

When everyone was done eating, Vero brought out some warm milk and some old packages of cookies. Sebastian saw his opportunity. He stood up, thanked Vero for the food, mumbled something about being tired, and made his way outside.

It was very dark outside. It seemed as though most the other houses had lost their lights as well. He stumbled on the uneven ground to the door of the room. He stepped inside and reached for the light switch, forgetting that it wouldn't work. It was even darker in the room. He pulled off his pants and shirt and found his way into a pair of shorts and a sweatshirt. He lay down under the covers of his bed, and stared, wide awake, at the darkness.

He noticed how darkness seemed to be made up of little dashing bits of color that fuzzed in front of his eyes. He didn't like how the darkness moved in front of him. He couldn't focus, so he closed his eyes, but he found the same darkness under his eyelids as well. He hated this darkness… all he wanted was a light. He opened his eyes and felt around for a flashlight. He knew there was one.

He found the neck of the flashlight with his hand, and he turned it on excitedly. Light seemed to flood the room when the weak beam shone faintly across the room. With the flashlight on, he lay on his back still wide awake.

He realized he had been sweating despite the damp cold. He realized that he didn't like being alone, just as he didn't like being with other people. Now that he could think, he didn't want to think. He closed his eyes and tried to sleep, but after a few restless moments, he heard the door open.

"Why did you leave?" Oscar's voice sounded different and Sebastian didn't like it. He opened his eyes and saw Oscar sitting on the twin bed that was next to Sebastian's. His eyes were round and sweet, as if he were a little boy again.

Feeling like an old man, Sebastian rolled onto his side away from his brother, "I was tired."

"Come on, Sebas. I really want to talk about what we've heard today."

"What did we hear?" Sebastian said, partly irritated and partly curious as to what Oscar had understood.

"About Jesus."

Sebastian grunted, "I didn't learn anything."

"Well, I was talking to Samuel. He explained everything to me, and, and..." Oscar's voice trailed off and Sebastian hoped he had changed his mind, but when Oscar's voice came back it sounded different, "I asked him to pray with me, Sebastian... And I don't know... I don't know anything, but, it was..." Sebastian turned around to see his brother. He didn't recognize this new voice, but when he turned, he saw something sparkling in Oscar's eyes in the dim light. They were tears. Oscar looked at Sebastian and finished his sentence, "It was real."

Sebastian was shocked and his eyes were glued to his brother's. He didn't know what to say, but he knew he didn't like this. He turned his eyes away from his brother, and he said somehow blurrily, "Oh, shut up."

"Please, Sebastian, listen to me."

"No!" Sebastian shouted and sat up in the bed. He surprised himself, but he wasn't going to stop. "I will not listen to you because you're being dumb. You're not being sensible."

"But God... "

"I don't care about God!" Sebastian roared out loudly. He realized everyone had probably heard him, but he didn't care.

Oscar just looked at him, he didn't look hurt or angry - he just looked calm, as if he was smarter. This irritated Sebastian even more.

"I don't understand you, Oscar," he said, "One day you're off getting drunk, and now you're listening to

God. You won't listen to our parents or to me, but now you come to this dumpy town and listen to some white guy talk about God and now you're going to be different? You're nuts, and I don't have to listen to you." He turned off the flashlight and lay back down on his bed.

He noticed a pain in his chest as he lay down again, he also noticed he was out of breath. He watched the darkness as he listened to Oscar undress and go to bed. Soon, he heard his brother's breath become heavy and he knew he was asleep.

He was no longer out of breath, but the strange little pain was still there. He couldn't sleep and he felt everything in him was tight. He thought he had already gotten his anger out, but he still felt as if he was going to snap in two. It irritated him that Oscar was sleeping peacefully, while he couldn't do anything but stare at the darkness and feel the tightness in his chest.

Eventually he fell asleep, though it felt as though it

was only his body. His mind was wide awake in a dream-world that terrified him. His dreams were full of his anger, his failures, and every insecurity he ever felt. He awoke early, with the distinct impression that even in his sleep, he couldn't escape himself. The anger had faded, and though his chest was still tight, he didn't feel like yelling. His feeling was simply melancholy.

Chapter 8 - The House on the Hill

That night Rosalía told Manuel about what Gregorio said and how they were expecting him at the church the next morning, but Manuel just stared at her blankly. It was useless, she knew, so she dropped it and began to remind herself to explain to Gregorio why Manuel didn't come.

The next morning, she was standing out by the *lavadero* and she looked up and saw the head and shoulders of the two men who were at church the night before, rising up over the edge of the hill. The oldest looked at her frankly, with his eyes in little slits, and the other approached her with a smile. "Hello," he said and extended his hand, "We came to pick up your cousin since he didn't come down to the church this morning."

"Oh, ok," she wiped her hands on her skirt, "I'll get him." She turned and began to walk toward the house. She could feel the eyes of the older one following her and tried to ignore the shivers going up her spine. "Manuel!" she said when she got to the open doorway.

In a few seconds, Manuel appeared in the doorway wearing blue jeans and a white tank top. His eyes were lazily rolling from Rosalía to the two men standing a few yards away from the door. His eyes widened a little. "What do they want with you?" he said to Rosalía in Mixteco.

"Nothing." she answered. "They're here looking for you."

"Me?" His eyes grew lazy again and he crossed his arms, trying to accentuate the small round muscles on his thin arms.

"Yes. They're the ones I was telling you about yesterday. Government men that want you to help them."

"Oh." he sighed and looked at the men for a second, then walked toward them. "Good day," he said in Spanish, "When do you need me to help you?"

"Right now." the oldest one said sharply.

"Right now?" Manuel asked causally.

"If you don't mind," the younger brother said, "We didn't mean to bother you or anything. We do this on a volunteer basis ourselves, but we really could use the help."

"Must you be so tactful?" the older one said to his brother and turning to Manuel he said, "Go put a shirt on and let's go."

Manuel didn't say anything more. He went back inside and came out again wearing a shirt.

Rosalía watched them disappear down the hill.

Before his shoulders disappeared, Manuel turned around, grinning slightly as he shrugged. She smiled at him.

The sun was hanging over the three peaks of the mountains above Cochoapa, ready to sink away to its resting place, but lingering as if it was waiting for someone to come home. Rosalía sat in the doorway humming to the baby in her lap. The lingering sun was shining on distant mountains. She could see that it was raining on those mountains and the rain was getting closer.

She looked over to see a head and shoulders appear coming up the hill. Manuel and the two other men came into her line of sight. They stopped when they got to the top. "Well, here you are," the younger man said to her cousin, "and we thank you very much." He looked over to her and waved slightly. The older brother stood behind him, looking less annoyed and more tired than he had that morning.

They turned to leave just as another head and shoulders appeared coming up the hill. It was that silhouette that Rosalía knew all too well.

Tío appeared before the men, his silhouette swaying as he tried to focus on the men, "Good evening!" he said, "How may I help you men?"

The younger brother said something that Rosalía couldn't hear.

"No, no, don't go yet," Tío said loudly, "Take her with you!" He began to stumble toward Rosalía.

She stood up, the baby in her arms, just as Manuel stepped in front of his dad, "Leave Rosalía alone, Papa." Tío grumbled something and Manuel grabbed him by the shoulders, and began to steer him to the door as she moved out of the way.

Manuel steered Tío inside and the men stood there watching. "Sorry," Rosalía said, "He's just drunk."

The light was fading away and a light drizzle began

as Rosalía stepped in her doorway and the men began to walk down the hill. She noticed the silhouette of the older brother turn slightly before he disappeared. She couldn't see his face but she could feel the glance.

It took a long time for Tío to finally go to sleep. For an hour, he stumbled around the room angry at Rosalía, angry at his wife – the very idea that Manuel stood between him and his mother and cousin infuriated him. Rosalía sat quietly with the small children, praying that Tío wouldn't hit Manuel like he had in the past. Eventually, Tío got tired and lay down on one of the blanket-covered, wood bed frames.

Rosalía lay the children down in their beds, then walked through the kitchen to the doorway. She sat down in the doorway, looking out at the silver drizzles of rain shooting through the darkness.

She heard a noise and jumped, but looked up to see Manuel, his body thin and his dark skin glowing yellow in the light of the lingering coals of the fire. "It's just me," he said and sat down next to her in the doorway.

They sat in silence with the dull warmth of the kitchen at their backs and the cold spray of the rain just out of reach of their faces.

"Thank you." Rosalía finally said.

"For what?"

"For always protecting us."

Even though she wasn't looking at his face and if she had, she couldn't have seen it clearly, she knew he had smiled. "It's his fault for having a son."

"What did you do today?" she said, resting her chin on her knees.

"We went all over town and hung dumb Draco Arroyo posters on all the posts and on half the walls. Like anybody really cares."

"Some people do." she mumbled.

"Those men are strange though," he said, "Sebastian and Oscar... They just fight the whole time. By what I can tell, the younger one became a Christian and is trying to convert the other one."

"Really?" She was surprised not at the salvation of the younger brother, but at the fact that Manuel was talking about it. Manuel cared a great deal about Rosalía but he didn't want to have anything to do with her god, or with any god.

"By what I can tell, Sebastian is mad at Oscar for becoming a Christian because now Oscar is nicer than he is. Sebastian says that Oscar is being a fake; he doesn't believe that someone can change that fast. He's convinced that Oscar is faking it, but Oscar just keeps talking about God. When he's not talking about God, he's reading a Bible. He even read parts out aloud while we were eating lunch at the church."

Rosalía was quiet, still surprised Manuel that would be talking about this. The last time she had tried to talk to him about God, he had told her angrily to never talk to him about it again.

"Oscar is really nice." he said after a few minutes. "He invited me to go to church with him next Sunday. I said I would go."

"Seriously?" Rosalía said, turning toward him in the dim light.

"Yes, seriously." Manuel grinned, "Don't get all excited. I'm not converted. I'm just going because he invited me."

"I've invited you before."

He laughed softly, "Yeah, but that's different."

It was different, she knew, but she couldn't help smiling a little as she turned to look at the rain again.

They stayed there silently for a little while longer, until Manuel stood up and stretched saying that it had been a long day and he was going to sleep. Rosalía was a little sad to see those moments end, but the small happiness of those minutes with Manuel lightened her heart a little. Manuel was by no means a perfect person. She often worried about the secret life he seemed to be living away from home. He was mean to his younger siblings and rude to almost everyone else. But he was never cruel to her; he was, on the contrary, quite gentle with her. After a few moments alone with the rain, she went to bed also, feeling comforted and maybe a little hopeful.

She lay down next to Teresa. She could feel the little girl trembling. "Rosalía?" the small voice whispered, "Rosalía, I'm scared."

She put her arms around the little girl, "Don't worry," she whispered, "God is with us, you can sleep in peace."

Chapter 9 – In the Rain

If it wasn't already annoying to have your brother peaching at you all day, he had to do it in front of a perfect stranger. Sebastian's anger festered deep inside; it had worn him down. As the light faded, he made his way back to the church with his brother where he retreated into himself to lick his wounds.

He hardly heard the small talk at the dinner table. He hardly heard his brother anymore, so when they went to bed, he just rolled over and closed his eyes. Although he closed his eyes, he didn't sleep. He lay still, listening to the rain on the roof, until he couldn't bear to be lying there any longer. He stood up, and then bent down feeling on the floor under the bed. He found it, the square shape of a book. He made his way through the darkness to the door with the book in his hand.

The lights had come back on that morning, so when he opened the door, light from a single bulb hanging from the overhang of the roof, blinded him. Beneath the light, next to the door, a wooden bench that was dry set against the wall. Sebastian sat down with his legs stretched out letting the silver rain drops hit his legs. He sat the paper-back Bible next to him but didn't open it. He watched the light reflecting off the rain drops, and looked at the little rivers of water running through the mud and rocks. He watched the rain running down his legs. He looked cold even to himself, but he didn't feel cold. He sighed through his nose, picked up the Bible that was next to him, and read the first thing he saw.

"The Lord is good. A stronghold in the day of trouble; And He knows those who trust in Him."

He put the book down. He felt cold now. He thought of going back inside, but no, he had to think it through or he would never be free. He had to figure out what it was about that simple sentence that perplexed him. He tried to think about it logically, but his thoughts didn't flow. He flipped through the pages again, "O, Lord, I have heard your speech and was afraid..."

He put the book down again and rested his head against the wall behind him. He watched the rain pouring off the overhang of the roof. Afraid. He guessed he was afraid. But it pained him too much to think of it. He was about to let his eyelids fall shut when he heard a noise and sat up straight.

Samuel was walking slowly, covered in a big rain coat, from the direction of the outhouse. Sebastian held his breath, but it was too late, he had seen him.

Samuel looked a little surprised. "Is that bench really that comfortable?" he asked with a funny little smile.

Sebastian didn't see what was funny about it, "No."

Samuel didn't keep walking as Sebastian hoped he would, he stood there, the rain pouring off his hood. "Are you ok?" he asked.

Sebastian didn't feel like telling the truth, but he didn't feel like lying either, "No." he said after a few seconds.

Samuel moved slowly and sat down a few feet from him on the bench.

"I don't understand what's happened to my brother. He was such a dumb kid when we came here, but now he's acting all religious."

"You think he's acting?"

"That's the only logical explanation."

He saw Samuel looking out at the rain, "Logical..." he mumbled, "Tell me: is your brother a good actor?"

"Only with girls." he said it without thinking. He didn't like talking to this man, but he found himself doing it.

Samuel laughed a little. But it didn't seem funny to Sebastian. "I don't understand," he said suddenly irritated at Samuel, "He was praying in that meeting yesterday. I.. I... don't pray. I don't think anyone would hear me. It's ridiculous. Not like I've never tried it before. I have. Nothing happens."

Samuel didn't say anything, he just continued to look out at the rain.

He found his mouth opening again, and he hardly heard his own words because of the pounding that had begun in his chest. 'Afraid', he thought for a split second before he began to listen to his own words,

"What you said made me feel bad. What you said made me think that my life is pointless… that everything is pointless and that I am a bad person. Life without the purity that I've felt here…life without this God, seems pointless. I don't like it. I don't like it." He heard his voice thinning as he ran out of words.

Samuel didn't look surprised, and he didn't apologize for making him feel bad. He didn't turn to him and tell him that he was a good person, like he wanted to hear.

"My family is Catholic. Everyone I know is Catholic or atheist. I never cared to think about it long enough to decide what I am. But I… I guess I need to decide what I am because I can't live like this. I can't live with this fear." He said it hardly caring about how weak he sounded. He knew he was weak, and he wondered if he would ever again find his strength.

"What is it that you don't understand?" Samuel said, glancing at him.

The question surprised him, he had been so lost in himself that he had hardly considered it. He thought for a long time, trying to gather his strayed thoughts into logical sentences. Samuel waited, showing no sign of becoming impatient. "Well, Jesus, I don't understand Jesus. I mean, everyone talks about him, and it's always been grilled into my head that he died on a cross, he died on a cross. But I don't understand. You were saying yesterday stuff about Jesus but I don't understand it. They all say that Jesus died for us," he paused, "But how did that help any? I mean, people still keep dying. And what about Mary? You people don't believe in Mary. You say you can talk to God directly, without Mary. I've confessed to the priest before – because I truly felt I needed to. That was hard enough, but if God is really all that you say he is, how could I ever talk to him and tell him stuff that I am ashamed of?"

Samuel seemed to wait a few minutes to be sure

Sebastian was done, then he took a breath, "Jesus was the one who took the punishment that we deserved. He did so because of love, yet, even love itself wasn't enough – it had to be a pure sacrifice of love. Jesus never did anything wrong. In all of history he was the only man who was able to keep every rule and law in every way. This combination of love and purity were acceptable to God.

He didn't just die, either. He rose again. He took all the punishment and still didn't die. People die because sin corrupted life, but Jesus died and rose again and now he offers us the purity and love of himself. That is, he offers us life. Not just on this earth, but eternal life. He offers life. He doesn't shove it down people's throats. That's why it's up to us to say yes or no."

Sebastian nodded but didn't respond for a long time. Finally, he asked a question that he had been wondering about since Oscar started talking to him, "So. If someone decides yes, what happens? What do they have to do?"

"Well, they don't have to do anything, really, just say yes."

"But my guilt –" Sebastian stopped then continued more softly, "What does one do about that? I will forever be changing my future, but the past can't be touched. What does one do about the past?"

"If we could do it ourselves, we wouldn't need Jesus. But the fact is we can't do it ourselves. There is no way to make up for what we've done. All other religions come up with ways to make up for your sin, but that's all a lie because in the end we can't make up for it. We're not strong enough." Samuel reached for the Bible that was sitting next to Sebastian.

As the American flipped through the pages, Sebastian felt a strange relief come to his thoughts. He didn't realize that it was ok to not be strong enough.

"*Come to Me, all you who labor and are heavy laden, and I will give you rest.*" read Samuel. He paused, "*If we* confess our sins, He is faithful and just to forgive us our sins and cleanse us from all unrighteousness." Again, he paused, "Let us therefore come boldly to the throne of grace that we may obtain mercy and find grace to help in the time of need."

Sebastian found himself leaning his head against the wall again, watching the rain and listening to every word Samuel read.

"It's not a pastor, or a priest, or Mary," Samuel said, "It's you and God alone. He wants to hear you, and I know for sure that He is more than capable of answering all the questions you have, of explaining it all to your heart in a way that no man can ever do."

Sebastian looked at Samuel and nodded once. Samuel stood up, and with a small smile he made his way back through the rain to his truck where he had been sleeping.

He was alone now, on the bench with his thoughts and with his heart. The rain seemed to be coming down harder. He stood up and began walking in the rain toward the outhouse. He wandered away from the light into the shadows. He was completely wet in a matter of a few minutes, but he didn't care.

He stood in the mud somewhere a few yards away from the outhouse. He looked up to the sky and the rain fell in his eyes. He closed them. He needed to talk. He couldn't stand it anymore.

"I'm here." he said, unsure if he said it out loud or not. "I don't know what you want with me, but you have my attention. I don't know if you're planning to ruin my life or what, but I can't live with this pain anymore." At that point, his throat tightened, "I can't live like this anymore."

Those were the last words he recalled having to force out, the rest just came out, not really in words, but in a burst of spirit and thought that he had never felt before. He had never really prayed before, and once he got the courage to say the name that he had so often heard, the

156

name of The One he knew was causing all this, he didn't want to stop. After that, he lost control of his mind and mouth, he was in a world where his heart was crying out, and what overpowered him most was the knowledge that possessed his heart that he was being heard. He trembled, and the water flowing down his face was no longer just rain. He knew what he was. He was a pitiful man, a weak man who had once thought so many thoughts, but now couldn't think of anything but a weak prayer to the God he had harshly rejected. He was a wordless beggar, and he wasn't even sure what he was begging for. He knew so clearly what a disgusting person he was. He felt pain. His tears mixed with the rain water.

"I don't need to come to my senses. I need to come to You." Of all the words he said, he said those clearly. His thoughts were nothing, his judgments were flawed, his life was dark all in comparison to the great purity of this Being that listened to him.

After some time, he didn't know how much time, his begging heart became quiet. Something in his chest was numb and tired. He realized what he felt, it was peace. It was inexplicable and quiet, but its silence was that which he had never before felt. It was as if everything was okay now. It was as if that terrible light had become soft and he no longer felt the guilt that had been hanging on his heart for so long. The purity was beautiful because he felt part of it inside him. 'No, no.' he thought, and he prayed again that this couldn't be. It couldn't be this simple, it couldn't be this easy. He needed to be punished, he needed to be pained. He couldn't just move on, could he?

Silence and an odd feeling of embrace were his only responses. He couldn't help but cry again. The peace in his heart was so full of words, but he couldn't think of one of them.

Slowly it all quieted again. He opened his eyes and realized he was on his knees in the mud with water running down every inch of his body. He stayed there, looking at himself. This wasn't normal, he knew, but something in him wanted it to be normal. He wanted to be there on his knees forever, but slowly he got up from the ground. He washed the mud off his knees with a bucket of rain water and walked back to the bench under the single light bulb. There was the paperback Bible, closed and dry where he had left it. But everything looked so different.

He changed into dry clothes and lay down on the bed. It was so soft and warm. In a few moments, he was fast asleep.

Chapter 10 – Brothers

When he first woke up he was unaware of anything except this own comfort. He opened his eyes and remembered what had happened. He felt a small twist in his gut – had it really happened? He lay there looking up at the wood beams under the tin roof thinking about the night before. Of course, it had happened. He was aware that he didn't feel empty like he had before. Yet he felt tight inside. What would he tell people?

"Good morning"

Sebastian jumped and turned to see his brother sitting up in bed. His hair was wild as ever, his eyes droopy with sleep, and a small smile on his lips. Sebastian felt a smile come to his lips as he looked at his little brother, he suddenly felt proud of him. "Good morning." he answered, aware that he was looking at his brother for far too long.

"Are you ok?" Oscar asked, a small laugh escaping him.

Sebastian nodded slowly and hesitated, he hadn't planned on having to say something so soon, but he couldn't stop it, and before he realized it, his eyes where wet. "I..." he started, his heart was beating like wild, "I'm sorry." he said, "I've been a very bad brother. I've been a bad example. You've followed my example and then...and then I just get mad at you for it. I've been such a bad person and I hated seeing you follow in my footsteps, but I hated it even more when you decided to be different." He could feel tears rolling down the sides of his face into his ears; it was very uncomfortable to have tears in his ears so he sat up.

Oscar looked shocked, "What happened?"

"God..." Sebastian said, unable to think of the words, "God got a hold of me last night."

"Seriously?" Oscar beamed.

"Yeah. I wasn't planning on becoming a Christian. I wasn't planning on praying... I was just...and He – boom!" It sounded so lame, he knew it, but there just wasn't an eloquent way of putting it.

Oscar let out another small laugh, and leapt out of his bed toward Sebastian. He caught hold of Sebastian and pulled him down into a great, half wrestling hug. "I'm so happy for you, brother!" His words muffled into the hug.

Sebastian smiled and wrestled himself free from his brother's grip, "But are you sure you forgive me?"

Oscar laughed and got up, "Of course!" He walked away toward where his clothes were piled on a chair. "I'm just so happy!" he said.

Oscar may have been happy, but Sebastian found himself unhappy in a strange sort of way. He was suddenly aware of everything around him, both beautiful and ugly, and the smallest thing brought to him a sense of deep guilt. The day went on and he found himself in chills when he saw Samuel and the others, he felt like he had to apologize for everything, for things no one even knew about.

After breakfast, they made their way back up to the hill. After what had happened the night before with Manuel's father, they weren't sure if they were welcome or not. The whole thing was confusing to Sebastian since much of what had been said had been said in the slurred Spanish of a drunk man.

They arrived and found Manuel waiting for them at the top of the hill. Sebastian found himself searching for the girl, Rosalía, but she wasn't there. He suddenly felt bad for the way he had treated her, though she was nearly a stranger to him.

The day was distinctly different from the day before, Oscar was chipper and Sebastian listened quietly, smiling at times. The boy, Manuel, was a quiet one, but he sensed an innocence under his tough act.

For the next few days they took their time hanging the posters, but very soon they ran out of posters and out of the desire to hang them. It was Friday afternoon when they realized they were done and didn't know what to do with their time. The three of them sat down in front of a little store with a cold Coca-Cola in a glass bottle that Sebastian had bought for them. They sat on old wooden chairs and looked out over the dirt street.

"You know," Oscar said, "This place grows on you."

Manuel looked at him a little confused. Tlapa was the farthest from home that he had ever gone. But Sebastian nodded and savored a mouthful of the cold bubbles, it tasted like the best coke he had ever drunk.

When they had gotten to the bottom of the bottles, the sun was caressing the tops of the mountains to the west. They walked up the hill to bring Manuel home for what they realized was the last time.

When they got to the top, Sebastian turned to Manuel, "You know, you really do deserve payment, it wasn't right to make you do this, without really asking if you wanted to. So, here," he pulled out his billfold and handed the boy a few green bills.

Manuel smiled at him oddly and took the money without saying a word.

Those nights were both the best and the worst for Sebastian. Some nights, he stayed up really late talking with Samuel or Gregorio. They talked about science, evolution, the Bible, and the meaning of life. Intellectually, it fascinated Sebastian, but internally, his heart would burn and sometimes his conscience would sting;

The moments he enjoyed most were the ones he spent with his brother. All his life he had his brother tagging along behind him, but he realized that he had never really known Oscar. Now, in the light of their new-found faith, he saw Oscar like he never had before. He saw that he was gentle and kind like their mother, and the he realized that he himself was like his father.

He noticed how Oscar was open and carefree about his new faith – he had no doubts or worries and his life had become so easy for him, but Sebastian was in a turmoil. He felt pangs of guilt and doubts nightly, and he realized his heart was not soft and tender like that of his mother and brother but that he was cold like his father. It frightened him. He would sometimes watch his brother speaking so unashamed about things he had only known for a few days and he found himself wishing he could be like his brother.

But he wasn't like his brother. Every night the conversations would end and the lights would go out and Sebastian would be alone again with the dark and his thoughts. Guilt for so many things he couldn't change would knot up his stomach. His mind would replay memories so vivid it was as if he was living them all over again. But those nights were an odd sort of delight because though he hurt, he didn't feel alone in the darkness. He could feel an indisputable presence that cut into the deepest darkest corners of his soul and saw it all. It was terrifying to know the things flashing behind his lids were not left unseen.

So, in the dark he would give up the struggle to hide and just let Him see. It was the only way to feel that peace he had known that first night. He always knew without doubts, the feeling so real like the touching of skin, that God had seen him. Just being seen and letting himself be seen, speechless before God, would loosen his tight muscles. He knew it was ok, and in that peace, he would fall asleep.

Sunday morning came, and Sebastian realized it hadn't even been a week since they had left home. He sighed as he got out of bed. Gregorio had talked to them a few days about baptism and he and Oscar had both decided that they did want to get baptized that Sunday after the meeting. Now the day had come and Sebastian realized what he was going to do that afternoon. He was going to admit to the world what he had felt in his heart.

They went to the wall-less meeting building with Gabriel. No one was there yet and Gabriel began to tune his guitar. A few old ladies came and then Sebastian saw Manuel and his cousin coming in the doorway.

Oscar jumped up and slapped Manuel on the back, "You came!" he said.

Manuel looked up at him, seeming a little confused, "Yes."

Oscar laughed, "Come with me."

He led Manuel to the front where Gabriel was with his guitar, and Sebastian stayed behind with the girl.

"Thank you for convincing my cousin to come." she said. "He never would come before."

"Oh, I didn't do anything. It was Oscar. But you're welcome."

The girl nodded, hesitated for a second, and then said, "Well, he must respect you guys very much, or else he would have never come."

"He shouldn't respect us." he said, looking down at the muddy cement, "At least, he shouldn't respect me. I'm just...human."

The girl smiled a tiny smile, "We're all human."

Sebastian smiled at her, surprised to see her smile, "Yeah I guess so." he said, "I know they told me before, but your name is...?"

"Rosalía." she said and held out her hand.

"Sebastian, nice to meet you."

After the meeting Gregorio announced that they
would be having baptisms and everyone was welcome to
join them. After a meal of beans and rice with the rest of
the church at long wooden tables carried into the wall-
less building, most of the young people in the church
joined them as they began to walk through town to the
other side where they would find the river.

Oscar walked with Manuel and Gabriel, who carried
his guitar on his back. Sebastian tried to walk along
with them, but found himself lingering behind. A group
of girls walked together as well, laughing among
themselves, but Sebastian didn't know what they were
talking about.

They walked down the road that lead out of town,
but then turned down some side streets that lead them
away from the main drag, and down a tiny dirt road. He

knew where he was until the houses slowly disappeared. The road turned into a trail that faded with every step into pine trees and down a steep hill on which he realized the whole town was resting.

The hill abandoned them with no more than three feet of flat land before the water of a tiny creek hurried its way past them. Then they turned to the right and followed the stream on its hurried way to the ocean. They arrived where the creek water was smooth and soft, and its color was a dark green. Gregorio stopped and smiled at Sebastian. "Here we are," he said.

Sebastian tried to smile. He stood holding a towel, feeling rather silly as Gabriel managed to climb up a huge bolder on the other side of the creek with his guitar on his back.

"There you have it! Our very own rock group!" Gregorio laughed.

Sebastian felt awkward, but he looked at his brother and found him smiling at everyone around him.

But when Gabriel started playing his guitar, and Gregorio started walking into the water, it somehow seemed both crazy and real at the same time.

"Boy the water's cold!" Gregorio laughed, and Sebastian realized he'd never seen him so happy, "Ok! Who's first?" He smiled up at them with the water half way up his thighs.

"I will." Sebastian said, though he thought Oscar would have beat him to it, but it didn't matter.

Gregorio smiled as Sebastian put his foot in the water. It was cold. It crept up his legs with every step and when he got next to Gregorio he was almost holding his breath because of the cold licking around his thighs. He tried to smile. His heart was pounding.

"Sebastian Arroyo," Gregorio's face was suddenly serious, "I have to ask you, have you accepted Jesus Christ as your Savior and Lord?"

Sebastian nodded, feeling he didn't have to think that question over too much. If that's all there was to it,

171

it seemed simple enough.

He had to duck a little under the water as Gregorio pushed him back. He was underwater for a second in which he didn't really know what he was supposed to be thinking, until he came out of the water. He came up out of the water with what felt to him like a great splash with water spraying out all around him. He could feel his skin tingling, wet with the cold water. His thoughts had seemed so clouded sometimes, but it came to him like the wind on his wet skin, the certainty and honor of what he had just done. This was his commitment, his sign, that God had broken into his stubborn heart and taken over. His heart was pounding and he smiled widely at Gregorio, and walked toward the shore where Vero stood holding the towel open for him. He reached her just in time to turn and watch his brother walking into the water.

Oscar walked in with his head held high, laughing at once at the cold water. When he got to Gregorio, he smiled widely at Sebastian and then took a deep breath.

Sebastian watched his brother go under with a great admiration for his little brother. He wondered if Oscar had clearer thoughts those few seconds under water, he wondered if he, too, felt the triumph of coming out of the water.

The wind, the babbling of the water of the rocks, the strum of the guitar, and singing from the people on the rocks seemed colorful to Sebastian, but that wasn't what had brought the feeling of joy in him. He knew very well that no human thing could cause what he had witnessed in himself and in his brother.

Oscar, too, seemed to burst out of the water in a magnificent splatter of water droplets. He walked out of the water toward Sebastian, his face glowing but twisted. He embraced Sebastian, surprising him with sudden affection. After a few moments, Oscar let go and Sebastian saw his brother wiping away tears as Vero put a towel around him.

A few minutes later, the crowd made their way back up the hill through the pine trees, but this time, Oscar and Sebastian walked side by side, with no one else. They walked in silence mostly, blissfully small smiles on their lips. They didn't notice the girls giggling and looking at them. They didn't notice Rosalía turning red at what the girls would giggle in her ear, they didn't notice Manuel watching them carefully, and they didn't notice Gabriel walking alone or Vero and Gregorio walking hand in hand. They walked together in silence. After years of brotherhood, they finally knew and understood that they were brothers.

Chapter 11 – Brave

The next day, they went to the mechanic shop where they had left their car. They had gone there several times in the last few days, thinking that 'any day now' would be that day. So far, the mechanic would only tell them to come back the next day, but that day when they went, the mechanic said that he had gotten the parts and the car would be ready the next day.

The wait finally ended and they would be going home soon, but when Sebastian heard that, he couldn't help but feel a little disappointed. The disappointment soon passed though, and was replaced with fear. He realized now that he would have to face his family very soon and that they wouldn't be happy.

He and his brother walked back to the church, Oscar seemed to be more excited, but his eyes were restless and Sebastian knew he must feel the same fear that he felt.

"It does seem incredible." Sebastian said as they walked slowly up the hill, "I mean, it's only been a week..."

"But, maybe we should take it slowly." Oscar answered energetically, "You know, not tell them right away."

"If it was fast for us, why shouldn't we break it to them fast? Besides, I think they'll know right away that something has happened... we don't act the same."

"Yeah, but that will actually help. They'll see our good character and kindness and then they'll be more willing to accept what has caused it."

"Maybe, but I don't think it will work that way. There will be a fight sooner or later. Not with Mom, but with Dad."

Oscar didn't say anything, but Sebastian could hear him breathing heavily.

"So that's the famous car." Vero said when he drove up in the car the next afternoon.

"It sure is," Sebastian said getting out and leaning on the hood.

"I bet you're glad to finally go home. You get to take a normal bath, eat good food, and see your friends and family."

"Yeah," he tried to laugh.

Vero's face softened, "But you'll miss us?"

Sebastian looked up, "Yes I will." He felt his eyes dampening and straightened up, hoping Vero wouldn't see.

But she saw, and swept him into one of her long hugs, "Don't you worry, Sebastian. I know this won't be easy, but we'll be praying for you ok? And your family and friends too."

"Thank you," Sebastian said, a little ashamed for the reddening of his eyes, but oddly relieved at Vero's affection.

He lay awake that night, staring at the darkness and smelling the distinct scent of pine on his skin from his last bucket bath. He knew he needed to sleep for the trip he and his brother would be taking the next morning, but some sort of nostalgia kept him awake. He had grown to love this place. It felt more like home than home now seemed. But aside from the distant nostalgia that was like the pine smell on his skin, there was something less foggy, and more real that kept him awake that night.

"Are you asleep?" His brother's voice interrupted his thoughts.

"No."

There was silence across the room for a moment, "Are you scared?"

"Yes."

"Me too." His voice continued in the darkness, "Everything's going to be different now. Everything is going to change."

Sebastian didn't answer and the minutes passed as he thought about what his brother said. He realized that his fear wasn't the same as Oscar's. He didn't have any desire for things to be the same as they were; he feared they would be the same. He was afraid of going back there and becoming exactly what he had always been.

He was afraid of seeing his family, afraid of seeing his friends, because they would treat him as though nothing had happened, and he would be tempted to be what he always had been.

He eventually fell asleep, but he didn't rest, his mind was occupied with his worries so much that it seemed when the alarm on his watch went off that he hadn't yet fallen asleep, though he knew by the sleepy feeling in his muscles, that he had slept.

He turned off his alarm and lay for a second looking at the gray light coming through the window.

The town was quiet in a blanket of fog as Sebastian and Oscar put their backpacks in the back seat of the car and turned to say goodbye. There were quiet promises of keeping in touch, of phone calls, of visits, but no one sounded excited. It was a solemn goodbye and soon over. Vero's quiet "We love you," seemed to hang in the white morning air.

They got in the cold car, and began to drive away, turning once to wave good-bye. A few people walked down the streets, mostly children on their way to school, but they were quiet and didn't do more than glance up at the passing car.

Oscar was curled up in the passenger seat asleep by the time they drove out of town and onto the curvy road. The way to Metlatonoc was so much shorter to Sebastian this time and when he got there he turned left, up the winding road that lead eventually to Tlapa.

He remembered how he had seen Cochoapa for the first time from this road. He watched for it as he drove along, hoping to catch one last glimpse of the town on that ridge, looking majestic in the sunlight as he had first seen it. But the fog hadn't yet lifted and he knew he had already passed it, unable to see it.

It saddened him, and now he knew the rest of the way wouldn't be anything special. He listened to the silence of the road and his brother's breathing as the sun burned all the fog away. He was well on his way now, passing through old ruts in the road and through splattered mud where he could now follow the tracks left by trucks through the bad parts.

The morning went on, and at the heat of the day they arrived in the hot desert towns. Oscar had woken up by then, but hadn't said anything in particular. No matter how much Sebastian tried to think of something to say, he couldn't think of anything. He gave up after a while and they spent hours starring ahead in silence.

Time seemed to pass so much faster as they passed through Tlapa and before they knew it, they were on the toll-road and it seemed so huge now.

It was late afternoon when they drove into the outskirts of Acapulco. The sight of the welcome sign and the familiar sights brought a sort of culture shock to Sebastian. It was so different.

They poured into the traffic and Sebastian's hands

seemed to be going numb from his grip on the wheel. He was shocked by the memories of the man who had driven out of the city in the same body that he was in now. It all came back to him, along with the thick Acapulco air: the stiffness of his thoughts in the early morning as he drove away, arrogant, angry, frustrated, thinking he knew better. Now what was he? He wasn't as strong; he didn't feel as sure, as confident. He was scared, scared when he once had been strong.

Maybe Christianity had weakened him. That thought came to him among the honking cars.

They passed through the city, making their way closer to the ocean. And suddenly there it was, laid out before them in blue: the Pacific Ocean. It was more beautiful than Sebastian had remembered.

They followed the road along the coast until they began to climb the slight hill at the end of the moon-shaped bay. Their neighborhood was quiet, as it almost always was. The large upper-class homes caged in with thick cement walls painted in bright colors with vines spilling over the tops were quiet. The streets were small and dirty, but had the solitude of riches. Sebastian felt like an intruder on those streets, though since his birth, these were the streets that were outside his bedroom window. He stopped in front of the gate of his house. He looked in past the curling metal bars, he noticed for the first time that the black paint of the gate was peeling away showing rust beneath it.

Oscar opened the gate and closed it behind the car as Sebastian drove in.

Sebastian turned off the motor after he parked behind his father's car. He got out, noticing first the ocean smell and second the smell of his mother's flowering plants that lined the inside of the walls.

He walked with his brother to the door, backpacks dangling from their hands, mud splashed a few inches up their blue jeans. Sebastian began to fumble for his keys but then the door swung open. He suddenly got a

burst of the smell of hard wood and scented candles –
the smell of his home.

"Sebastian Arroyo!" his mother said, "I was worried
sick about you!" She threw her arms around his neck,
"Why didn't you call? It's been over a week since you've
called, didn't you see all my text messages?"

She let go and embraced Oscar for a long time as
Sebastian said, "Forgive us, Mama, I...I guess we forgot.
And I haven't turned on my cellphone. It didn't work
there so I turned it off. And, I guess I forgot about it
after that."

She let go of Oscar, "Sebastian," she looked him
straight in the eyes, "I am your mother. There is no
excuse not to call."

He realized her seriousness when he noticed the
dampness in her eyes. She turned and they went inside
the house together, "Is Dad upset?"

"No," she sighed, "He said you're a grown male adult
and you were working. But he's not your mother. Put

that junk down, come on, we'll find you some food."

They walked past their living room and into the large kitchen. "Where's Dad?" Oscar asked, propping himself up on a familiar bar stool.

"In his office talking on the phone. Busy, busy." She smiled at him, "I missed you so much."

She went on talking about Fatima's mother and all the things that had happened among her friends and her son's friends when they were gone as she moved about the kitchen, frying up familiar smells. "Fatima's brother – you know, the older one that went off and joined the army... "

"Cristofer." Oscar filled in.

"That's the one!" she said, "-is having a party of sorts at their house this weekend, I guess it's some birthday thing or something. Anyway, Fatima called me. Said she'd been texting you to invite you but you never answered. I told her you'd be back by today. (What a lucky guess, huh?) I promised her you'd come. She's especially looking forward to seeing you, Sebastian." She grinned.

"Oh." he said, unsmiling. He had forgotten about his little game with Fatima.

"What's wrong, Sebastian?" his mother smiled, "Aren't you excited to spend some time with her?"

Before he could answer his father came in to the kitchen behind them. "Sebastian. Oscar," for a moment it seemed as if he was going to hug them but instead he stood in front of them, with a wrinkle on his forehead.

"Hi, Dad." Sebastian said, and smiled as best he could. He could feel his father's eyes observing him closely. He didn't know how to act because he didn't remember how he acted before.

"How did it go?" his father watched him, "What did you do?"

"It went good." Sebastian said then took a breath and was going to continue, when his mother cut in.

"Now leave them be, Draco. They're tired and hungry

and they have a party to go to tonight." she winked at Sebastian.

"Tonight?" Oscar asked.

Sebastian watched his mother. He knew what she was doing. She was defending her sons and protecting them from her husband as best she could. He realized that she had always done that. Suddenly, he realized like never before how much he loved his mother. He just wanted to make her happy, but, he sighed, "We're not going to the party," he said, leaning wearily against the counter.

His mother looked at him strangely, "I was just joking, it's not that important. But, it wouldn't hurt any to go."

"It is important... It's important that I tell you that I'm not going to those parties anymore." He turned and faced his father, "I need to tell you what we did, Dad."

Oscar looked at Sebastian with panic in his eyes.

"What do you mean?" Draco said, narrowing his eyes

at his son.

"Dad, we stayed at that church, you know, and the people were very nice to us. We went to their meetings and, well, on Sunday we were baptized. We're Christians now."

Drusilla turned pale. She looked at Sebastian in shock for a few seconds, but he looked away from her and watched the gray shadows of the tiles of the floor. He had spoken too soon, too frankly, hadn't he? He glanced up at his father's face. It was white, quickly turning red.

"You're *what* now?" Draco said hoarsely.

"I know it sounds crazy. Just let us talk. Let me tell you what I felt."

"What you felt? I don't care what you felt." his father spewed out his words.

"I just need you guys to understand that I'm different now, and I'm not going to be the same as I always was. I hope you'll be able to understand." he watched his parents carefully.

Drusilla started to nod, but Draco looked at his son seemingly calm, "No." he said, "You know you can do whatever you want outside this house, but you can't live in my house, eat my food, and be a Christian and expect me to understand."

"Draco," Drusilla said gently and reached for his arm.

"No." he simply said, "If you have any intention of living in my home and carrying on the Arroyo family position, you will not be a Christian. Take back everything you've said, renounce it all now, pretend it was a joke, and we'll move on." He clapped his thin hands together and looked at Sebastian.

Sebastian looked at Oscar who had remained seated and quiet the whole time, watching his brother with round eyes. He looked at his mother whose eyes were wet and face was pale, and his father whose eyes were bulging, but his color was restored. This was his family, this had been his home, yet he noticed that his heart was beating in a way that made him feel like a stranger despite his familiar surroundings.

"I won't." he said, like a sigh. "I won't pretend. I can't move on. God's done something in me." he watched his father's eyes and saw heartbreak in them, "I'd really like to tell you about it," he added.

Suddenly his father's face turned red again, "Don't tell me." His calmness left him, "You can say good-bye to your inheritance, your college education, your stuff, your home, your family because you are no son of mine if you change your religion and then talk about 'telling me'. You don't tell your father – I am your father! I know more than you, I've lived longer than you! I've seen Christians and my son will not be one of them!"

His father's face inches from his own, Sebastian stared in shock.

"Draco," his mother said, breaking into the few-inch gap between them. "Calm down."

"I won't calm down!" he shouted at her, backing away from her and Sebastian. "Get out Sebastian!" He didn't look at anyone, and turned toward the back window, "Get out!" he whispered.

Drusilla stood starring at her husband's back in disbelief. Sebastian looked at Oscar, unsure of what to say or do.

"Dad," he walked toward him.

"Pack your bag, Sebastian. You're not welcome here."

He stepped back. He looked at his mother. She wouldn't look at him. Oscar looked at him, but his eyes didn't give away clues about his feelings. Sebastian turned and left the kitchen. He passed outside the doorway and picked up the backpack he had dropped there on his way in. As he did so, he heard his father ask Oscar, "Now, Oscar, how did you spend your time there?"

There was silence, then his brother's voice answered

quietly, "It was a joke..."

"Draco!" His mother's voice broke in, "You can't do this. He's our son, he will always be our son, he will always be welcome here!" her voice cracked.

Sebastian's throat tightened and he left with his backpack in his hand. He went past the living room, to the pine staircase and made his way upstairs. He opened the door to his room and walked in. There it was. Neat as a pin. His books on the bookcase by his desk. His bed made up neatly and not one thing out of place. He saw himself personified in his belongings. Neatness, intelligence, and seriousness. Something in him melted when he saw himself here. He sat down on the edge of the bed. He needed to think, he needed to understand. What did he expect? What did he think? What did he feel? Could he just go back to his dad and say he was sorry and he would never talk about it again? Could he leave? Where would he go? He looked around his room remembering his friends, his relatives, thinking maybe they would take him in until his dad changed his mind. His eyes wandered down to the Caterpillar boots on his feet, still covered in dried mud. He knew. There was only one place where he would be welcome.

He stood up, and pulled a small suitcase out from under his bed. He opened it and looked around the room. He put his hands on his face, this couldn't be happening. But it was. He looked around the room again and began to take out things. He took out his favorite clothes, including some nice ones, as well as his dress shoes. He pulled out a few of his law books and notebooks half-full of homework and notes, as well as a few paperback novels he had liked when he was younger. He paused and looked at them, they were adventure stories. He took the money and personal papers he had. He zipped up the suitcase, put his backpack on top of it, and looked around one last time. He turned toward the window. He opened the sliding glass door and stepped onto the balcony. There it was again: the ocean, in all its splendor. He had been on that balcony a million times, but it seemed to him that it had never been more beautiful than it was at that moment.

His heart was pounding wildly in his ears. He didn't want to leave. He wanted to curl up in his bed. What if he woke up and found his old self back? Maybe the old owner of this room would return and go back to his life? No. He didn't want that. What if he woke up the next morning to find his father changed his mind? The thought gave him a little hope; he took a deep breath of the salty air. He went in his room and picked up his back pack and suitcase. He didn't look around one last time. Instead, he pushed his nostalgia aside. Surely this goodbye wouldn't be forever.

He closed his bedroom door, and as he turned, he saw Oscar coming up the stairs. Fear suddenly rushed through him when he saw his brother's grin. Why was he grinning?

Oscar came closer and stopped, "So, you're not going to the party, huh?"

"No." he said, barely hearing his own voice.

Oscar grinned again.

"What are you so happy about?" This time he heard his own voice loud and clear.

"Oh, I'm not happy." he wrinkled his forehead as if on purpose. "I hate to say it, but I told you so. You needed to take it slowly. Pretend you're not a Christian. We have too much here to just give it up. I mean, no college education, no spending money, no respected family name? That's too much to give up."

"I can't pretend. It's too real to pretend. What you pretend you eventually become – you have to be careful, Oscar."

"I know. I have to be careful and make sure no one finds out about this."

Sebastian caught a glimmer in Oscar's eyes, like a

memory of the Oscar he seemed to have left in Cochoapa, but the glimmer left and Oscar looked away. "Look," he said, "I love you and all that, but the truth is: If you're gone, there's more for me. I'll let you know, though, I'll let you know if dad changes his mind." He shrugged, "I suppose you're going back."

Sebastian's throat was tight, he wasn't sure if with anger or sadness, "Yeah, well, I have nowhere else to go." he mumbled.

"Good luck," Oscar punched him quickly in the arm and, avoiding eye contact, headed toward his own room, across the hall from Sebastian's.

It took him a few seconds to be able to pick up his suitcase and move toward the stairs. His stomach was a knot as well as his throat, and his feet were heavy like iron.

He made it down the stairs, in short stiff steps, trying to be as silent as he could, trying to think of what to say now that he was forced to say goodbye. But he didn't have much time to think because he soon saw his mother waiting for him at the bottom of the stairs.

She saw her son coming down the stairs and looked down, her hands clasped in front of her. She was silent when he got down the stairs. He stood there, looked down at his mother, waiting for her to say something. Finally, he took a deep breath and was about to say something, when she spoke first, "When you were gone I was going through your baby pictures and pictures of when you were a kid. I thought I'd give you some." She handed Sebastian a small stack of pictures, but wouldn't look at him, "You were so sweet..." she said, her voice trailed off into silence.

"Mama," he sighed, "I'm sorry."

She looked up, "Oh, Sebastian. Don't be sorry. Your dad just... feels very strongly." Her makeup was smudged and her face wrinkled anxiously, "Couldn't you just... I mean?" She put her face in her hands, and

Sebastian reached to hug her, but then she looked up at him. "You're just like him."

Sebastian opened his mouth, indignant that she should say that he was like his father at a time like this. His only desire these last days was to never be like his father.

"His faith is strong, Sebastian." she explained, knowing her son well enough to see his thoughts, "But I see that yours is too. Like your father, you're being brave for standing up for what you believe and not backing down. You're very brave, as is he. I just wish you could both be on the same side."

"But mama, I'm not just trying to be stubborn or contrary. Something really great happened to me that was out of my control. It wasn't me. I promise it wasn't me. And brave... I'm not sure what that is, but I'm sure that I'm not. It's still not me. All this is more than me."

Drusilla's eyes narrowed, as if she was trying hard to understand, "I respect your new faith." she said finally, "But your dad doesn't."

"I know."

"Have you ever thought maybe you should respect his?"

"But, I'm not trying to be disrespectful... Here," he unzipped his backpack and pulled out the paperback Bible, "Read it."

Drusilla smiled like mothers do at gifts from a small child. "Ok."

"Please, Mama."

She narrowed her eyes again, "Ok." she repeated.

"Where's dad?"

"Oh, he's in his office."

"Can I go see him?"

"You probably shouldn't bother him..."

"But I want to say goodbye to him. He's still my father." He started walking toward the office. By the front door was the small room that was his father's office. He found the glass door closed, and saw his father inside, pacing back in forth as he shouted on the phone. His words were muffled, but he could hear a word here and there and Sebastian knew he was talking about him.

He raised his hand to knock. Drusila touched his arm, "Sebastian, don't. Just leave him alone."

Just then he saw his dad glance up and see him, then quickly look away.

"I'll talk to him when you're gone. He might come around with time."

Sebastian nodded and turned toward the door, suitcase and backpack in hand. He opened the door and stepped outside, "Well, I guess this is goodbye." he said and turned towards his mother. Her face turned red and in an instant, she was in his arms, mumbling and sobbing into his shirt.

He found himself holding his mother like a child in his arms. The hope that had carried him out the door faded away and he realized his world was gone. It was over. He felt he had to be strong for his mother, that he had to be brave like she said he was.

But he didn't feel brave or strong as he finally turned from his mother and walked stiffly, with tears in his eyes down the small driveway. When he got to the gate he turned and saw his mother standing at the door watching him. He saw her put her hands to her face. He turned and went out.

The streets were quiet, and he didn't remember ever walking down them before, only as a boy had he played in the streets. He felt like that little boy, small and running away from home after disagreeing with his daddy.

His thoughts were long and consisted mostly of exhausting memories that made every minute drag reluctantly into the future. With this frame of mind, he found a taxi. He rode in the back seat watching the city of Acapulco move past the window. It was alive with color, pulsing with a mixture of old and new, of speed and tranquility. It was not new to Sebastian, but he saw it with new eyes. Now it seemed to fascinate him like it never had before.

His heart ached. He realized it as the city faded behind his tears. The color blurred together like a melancholic abstract painting. He realized now, without confusion, without bravery, but also without regret – the pain. It was a nearly physical twisting in his heart and he didn't care if the taxi driver glanced at him in his rear-view mirror.

The taxi driver left him in front of the bus station. Buses, vans and taxis were coming and going all around him. He sighed. His cheeks were no longer wet, but had on them the feeling, like a shell on his skin, of dried saltwater.

He stood in line, everything inside him very still as the world moved around him. When he got up to the window he bought a ticket to Tlapa de Comonfort on the first van that went there. The man behind the counter didn't look up as Sebastian spoke quietly and handed him the money.

There were two hours yet before the van would leave for Tlapa. The terminal was crowded and he looked around at the filled seats of people waiting. There were empty seats, but he was drawn outside by the desire to get a last glimpse of his city and by the growling of his stomach.

He walked down the street with his heavy suitcase in his hand. "Tacos, tacos, tacos!" A woman shouted on the corner. There he leaned against the wall with a small crowd of people and ate tacos he bought from the lady.

With his stomach full the world seemed like a better place. He knew he had done the right thing. He walked around the block, though he felt silly dragging around his suitcase, but he remembered having seen some sort of book store around there.

He finally found a door that could have been mistaken for a door to an apartment on the street if it wasn't for the big white letters painted above it on the wall, *Libreria Cristiana.* Sebastian smiled to himself, it was a book store, a Christian book store.

A small bell went off when he pushed the door open. The smell of dirty carpet filled his nostrils. There was a girl standing behind a counter. He smiled as best he could, but she didn't smile back. She looked at him closely as he walked slowly, carrying his suitcase. There were very few books in the book store and most of them were just Bibles, but that was really all he had come to look for. He knew the girl was watching him closely as he picked up several Bibles, looking at them. In a few moments, he chose a black leather Bible in the same version that they had given him in Cochoapa.

He held the Bible he had chosen in his hand and tried smiling at the girl again, her face was motionless.

He looked at his watch. He still had an hour. He sighed and looked around him. There was a shelf with books that weren't Bibles. He didn't bother trying to smile as he carried his suitcase to that side of the room. All the titles on the shelf begged to be read. He had never known there were so many books written about Christianity.

After half an hour of flipping through books, he made his way to the counter with the Bible and a copy of C.S. Lewis' *Mere Christianity*. The girl looked him up and down, but said nothing but the price.

He made his way back to the bus station feeling somewhat encouraged. His heart still ached, and he doubted that would ever go away, but his feet knew their direction and didn't drag on the pavement.

The van made its way out of the city with Sebastian sitting at the window behind the driver. The sun was setting beautifully over the ocean. As he was watching it, he suddenly remembered his cell phone. He picked up the backpack at his feet and found it in one of the pockets, off, like he had left it in Cochoapa. He took a breath and turned it on. A few seconds later, it vibrated and buzzed in his hands, notifying him of missed calls and unread messages.

He read them all, texts from Fatima, his mother, and countless other friends. Invitations, jokes, flirtations. His Facebook overcrowded with pictures of girls and dirty jokes. He went to the music on his phone, wanting to console himself with music, but he found nothing on his phone that was worth listening to anymore.

As they left the city, and the signal on his phone got weaker and finally disappeared, Sebastian felt a sharp pain – ashamed of the man that owned that cell phone. But realizing that he had no one to call anymore, suddenly the pain went from shame, to a quiet loneliness.

Chapter 12 – If the Mountains Could Talk

He was awakened from a sound sleep as the van lurched, bumped and finally stopped. He squinted into artificial light as the people around him began to dismount. He somehow dragged himself and his suitcase to a hard bench in the Tlapa station. For the next two hours, he sat on a hard bench, half asleep with the sound of the TV being too loud to ignore and too low to understand. The lights were too bright; he could see them when he closed his eyes, but when he opened them, he couldn't see anything because they blinded him. His thoughts were asleep and unable to awake, so they were of no interest to him. He was aware of nothing but the fact that he couldn't stay awake and he was too awake to fall asleep.

Six o'clock finally came around and he found his way into the back seat of a small Nissan truck. It was comfortable enough at first to snooze the time away, but soon it became more cramped with the filling of more people at its stops along the road. Soon he realized that the cab was filling with women and children and it was only right that he should make room for them. So, he got out of the comfortable seat and climbed into the back where he found mostly men standing and holding on to the metal frame.

He stood toward the front, looking ahead into the cold wind. It was a cold morning, and even as the sun rose, it was blocked by heavy clouds. His hands and face grew numb from the cold wind but his mind woke up and he realized that despite the cold and numbness, and the tiredness of his legs from standing, stiff and firm against the movement of the small truck, it was an exhilarating way of traveling. The mountains were vivid and beautiful, even in the light of the clouded day. His thoughts moved and flowed as if the wind was clearing his thoughts as well. He knew he had done what was right, and though it wasn't happiness that he felt, he did feel freedom. He knew that he had given up the comfort and security most desire, but he knew also that he had chosen the adventure that comes along with uncertainty.

Some go through a journey anticipating the arrival, only to realize when they arrive that the journey was the best part. That's what Sebastian realized when he finally arrived in Cochoapa. He was trembling. He didn't know if it was his emotions or the vibration of the vehicles he had been in for the better part of twelve hours.

He walked up the main street, suitcase in hand and backpack on his back, knowing that the eyes of the town watched him. He tried to think about what he should tell Gregorio and Vero, realizing it would have been better if he had called them and they had known about his coming. He avoided mud puddles. He hoped he wouldn't see anyone he knew, but then he realized he didn't know that many people.

Vero was startled, to say the least, to find Sebastian standing at her door the day after he had left. But Gregorio seemed to take his return in a way that made Sebastian think he had expected it. "Where's your brother?" he asked.

Sebastian shook his head, and Gregorio's eyebrows rose.

An hour later, Sebastian was sitting at the kitchen table, an empty plate and coffee mug in front of him. Across from him sat Vero with her head in her hands, and Gregorio with his forehead wrinkled.

"I don't understand how he could do that so easily," Sebastian said, "I can't help but worry that I did the wrong thing. That I am being silly, that all that we went though was just a dream or an illusion... but no, right? It was too real. It wasn't a dream. I believe in salvation because I've known it."

"You say that like you're trying to convince yourself." Gregorio said rubbing his chin.

"I guess I am... but that's what is so confusing... what happened to Oscar? Is he not saved anymore? Was he never saved?" he looked at Gregorio helplessly.

Gregorio sighed deeply, "Well, Sebastian, that's a question that has been asked lots of times. Some people hold the belief that a person cannot lose their salvation, while others think it can be lost. I have seen many cases... and I wonder sometimes. For example, I knew a guy who was miraculously healed of cancer and became a Christian because of that." He had a faraway look in his eyes, and the wrinkles of his forehead told of a pain that was much greater than the steadiness of his voice would ever betray. "In a few years, he had started living in a wild, uncontrolled way, and he wasn't sorry. It seemed like overnight, he went from being a good Christian, to losing it. But we who knew him best, we had seen that he had sins in his heart that he pampered. He kept up a good outward appearance for a long time, but in the end, everyone knew and by that point he was too cold to be changed by any of us." He shook his head as if trying to shake a memory away, "See, what happens is that if we ignore the Holy Spirit's convictions long enough, we will lose it. And if we go on this way, never repenting, we lose it all. It says in the book of Ezekiel that if a wicked man turns from his ways, his wickedness will no longer be remembered, but that if a righteous man turns from righteousness and does wickedness, his righteousness will no longer be remembered.

Now, when it comes to your brother, I think he's just now at the first step. He's ignoring the conviction of the Holy Spirit."

"So, you think he really did become a Christian – he wasn't just pretending?"

"Well, I think so. I saw him, I heard him... but of course, we don't know for sure. You know your brother best; you should know more than anyone."

Sebastian nodded, but said nothing.

He found himself in the same room where he and Oscar had been for the last week, but this time he unpacked his suitcase, putting his things in the old closet that stood in the corner.

Beginning the next morning, he joined Gregorio in the carpenter shop. He knew nothing about that work. The feel of wood under his hands and the handling of the loud machinery was a new experience. In a few days, he learned the basics, and began to work in silence with Gregorio for hours on end.

He knew he had to earn his keep, he knew he had to work and be useful, but that wasn't what motivated him. His hours of silence were a refuge for him. It was during these hours when his mind focused on the work of his hands that his mind rested from its worries.

At night, he would lay awake for hours, wondering what he was doing there, what his brother was doing, and if it was real. He tried to pray, but his prayers were endless rummaging of doubts and fears. He felt exhausted, and often fell asleep in mid-prayer. In the morning, he was unsure again, whether he had been heard.

About a week after his return, Samuel was expected to return from Oaxaca to visit again. Sebastian found himself waiting for him, glancing out of the work-shop doorway, waiting for the big, white truck to pull in. He didn't know what he would say to Samuel and he dreaded having to explain his presence. Yet, he craved some affirmation of his convictions, as well as comfort and some sort of wisdom concerning his brother.

When the truck drove in, Sebastian wasn't expecting it. When he looked up from his work, the truck was pulling in, and Gregorio had already walked to the doorway and was grinning.

"Sebastian!" Gregorio's mouth moved.

He nodded and turned off the cutter and it whined one last time.

He stood with the family as they greeted Samuel.

"Sebastian – what are you doing here?" Samuel said.

"Long story," he said trying to smile as he shook his hand.

That night at the dinner table, the whole story was drug out again, mostly re-told by Vero and Gregorio with a few clarifying details from Sebastian. It was one of those nights when the lights went out and they saw each other in candlelight. Samuel's eyes were narrowed in seriousness. When the story came to an end, no one said anything. They sat watching the candlelight making shadows on the wooden walls.

Samuel stepped outside after dinner and Sebastian stepped out after him. A very light rain had just stopped falling and its remains were running off the roof.

"Samuel?" Sebastian asked, making him stop and turn to face him. "Do you think my brother really did become a Christian? I ask because, well, you knew him best when he was here."

He nodded slowly, looking somewhat uncomfortable, "I think he was, Sebastian."

His heart sank, "Oh." he nodded, "But is he now?"

Samuel leaned against the wall, letting the rain water from the roof splash down his raincoat. He looked pensively for a moment, "Some things we can't know," he said, "I understand why this is hard for you because he is your brother, but you have to stop worrying about him. If he is still saved, God will show him what he has done wrong. If it's that he faked it from the beginning, we ourselves need to learn not to fake it, but to be real before God and others. If it's a case of lost salvation, we need to take warning from it and watch ourselves. But, Sebastian, whatever the case may be, beating yourself up about it won't help."

That night Sebastian stayed up late, thinking about what Samuel had said. He took out his Bible and looked up Ezekiel, trying to find the place Gregorio had quoted the day he arrived. He found himself reading most of the chapter, but the part Gregorio had quoted wasn't the part that stood out to him most, '...*When the watchmen sees the enemy coming, he sounds the alarm to warn the people. Then if those who hear the alarm refuse to take action, it is their own fault if they die. They heard the alarm but ignored it, so the responsibility is theirs... But if you warn them to repent and they don't repent, they will die in their sins, but you will have saved yourself.*'

"Save yourself." he whispered. That's what he had to do. Oscar knew the truth and Oscar was responsible now. What Sebastian had done in leaving Acapulco was just that, saving himself.

He slept better that night, though in the days that followed, he began to wonder what it meant to be a watchman.

The last time Samuel had been there he had gone to

another village with Gregorio and another man from the church. Sebastian didn't think much of it the time before, and this time Gregorio again invited him to go with them. Although he didn't know exactly where they were going, or what they would do when they got there, but he didn't ask.

Church on Sunday was partly miserable, and partly wonderful for Sebastian. It was good to be there, but yet he knew he stood apart from everyone else and he knew they were watching him. He blocked it out of his mind though, and instead sat in the front with Gabriel and his guitar.

When the meeting was over, Sebastian looked behind him and saw what had been part of his misery. He saw Manuel, sitting hunched over next to his cousin. He stood up and walked toward him, his face still. "Where's Oscar?" shaking his hand.

"He's not here."

"Why not?" Manuel looked at him blankly.

Sebastian explained slowly, trying to spare him the details, but Manuel's blank eyes went stony, revealing that the Indian mind was not as empty as Sebastian had once thought. "But that doesn't mean you should give up on God because of Oscar's mistakes. God knows about Oscar," he took a deep breath and looked at Manuel. A little shy in saying what he was about to say, but he said it anyway: "And He knows about you too."

He tried to read Manuel's eyes for some expression, some feeling, thought, or sign of understanding, but he found none. Manuel left without saying goodbye a few moments afterward.

After lunch that day, Samuel and a man from the church leaned over rolls of maps spread out over the kitchen table. Antonio, he learned, was the name of the man that leaned over with Samuel, nodding and grunting in a shy Indian way. He didn't look very special to Sebastian; he was short with a sleepy look in his eyes like most Indian men. He wore a sparse attempt at a mustache on his upper lip, and when he spoke, he spoke with long pauses and grammatically incorrect Spanish.

On Monday morning, he stood in the fog, wrapped in his jacket, as they got themselves together and finally loaded themselves into the white truck. He shivered on the cold, vinyl seat covers with Gabriel and Gregorio. Antonio sat in the front with Samuel.

They drove in silence, a few heads dropping into sleep. They drove toward Metlatonoc, but before they got there, they turned right on a little dirt road and that was the last time Sebastian knew where he was.

In a few hours, the sun had burnt the fog away, revealing the huge valleys and mountains around them. Crisp greens and tiny towns lacing the mountains met Sebastian's eyes.

In the fresh sunshine, they stopped and ate

breakfast. They ate Samuel's favorite tuna with *chipotle* and beans out of tin cans on *tostadas*. As they stood and munched on the side of the road, kicking rocks around under their feet, Samuel pointed to a mountain, the highest in sight but only slightly, "*Cerro de la Garza*" he told Sebastian, "That's where the people go make sacrifices."

"Sacrifices?"

"Turkeys, goats sometimes."

"To what?"

"Saint Mark, god of the rain – that's the big one. But they go up there for lots of other things too."

Antonio nodded, "Mmm, they ask for healing or things like that?"

"But saints..." Sebastian started.

"Oh, here Catholicism and spirit worship are kind of mixed together," Samuel said.

"Spirit worship?"

"Mmm," Antonio grunted again, "Witchcraft."

They kept munching as the early morning breezes channeled themselves through the mountains.

Witchcraft; sacrifices; Sebastian looked up at the round tip of that mountain above. A strange panic rushed into him, gripping at his stomach. He realized that he didn't know why.

Soon they were rumbling down the mountain again, and Sebastian's thoughts bounced around with the truck. Sure, the people here believed those things and did witchcraft – but it was a rootless belief. He tried dismissing it from his mind. They were ignorant people. They believed in evil spirits because of ignorance, he told himself.

It seemed to take most of the day, but it was really only about noon when they got down to the valley. The town was crowded and tiny, sitting numbly at the edge of a wide brown river. It was hot. His sweatshirt was off long before arriving, and now his shirt was sticking to his back.

He began to sweat even more after they parked on the basketball court in front of the small presidency building and they began to unload bags of used clothes from the back of the truck and spread the clothes out on tarps on the ground. A crowd gathered quickly after an announcement was made in Mixteco over the loudspeaker. The people stood around looking at them curiously, whispering among themselves, until Antonio stood in front of them, with a Bible in his hand, and began to talk to them.

He guessed what he was saying was about God, but he understood no more than a few words in Spanish that seemed out of place in the speech he was making.

The sun beat down on him as he stood and listened to the words he didn't understand. After Antonio finished, a sort of chaos broke out when the people were told to take the clothes. Then Sebastian found himself official distributor of candy to the kids. He was on the ground next to a box of old candy, handing it out by the handfuls to a crowd of kids pushing against him and holding out their hands.

When it was all over and there were only a few ties and pair-less shoes on the tarp, Sebastian thought they would be leaving, but then he saw Antonio with a box and he knew it wasn't over yet. He saw the real reason for this trip unfold when Antonio produced from the box not only Bibles in Spanish, but things in Mixteco: the Jesus movie on DVD, booklets and CD's of some books of the Bible in Mixteco.

He sat next to Gabriel on the tailgate of the truck, partly in shade from the sun as they watched and listened to Antonio talking to the people and pointing into booklets. He realized that Antonio was the most important part of the group. Gregorio could speak a little of the language, and Gabriel spoke it fluently even though he didn't speak much at all, but Antonio, aside from being able to speak the language, he had a way with talking to the people. He knew the people because he was one of them, and the people listened to him.

They left when the sun was lingering above the highest mountain. They were all talking more, Antonio telling them about what someone had said and how he had answered, Gregorio nodding from the back seat, and Samuel asking him what he had told the people at a certain time.

The sun was beginning to dip when they stopped for an afternoon meal of beans and tuna, when a man came walking up the road toward them. Antonio seemed to know him, and as he came walking up the muddy road, he stopped him and offered him a cup of Pepsi and some food. He was an ordinary Indian man in every way except for a look in his eye that made you think that he couldn't really see you with his eyes, or that the man's eyes weren't what was looking at you. Maybe it was only a glazed over expression, so Sebastian thought it away. All Indian people seemed to have this look, he decided.

But as he noticed how he answered Antonio when he talked to him – he noticed that he wasn't simply distracted or shy, but he was mentally imbalanced. He spoke haltingly, often not making much sense, distracted, yet not avoiding eye contact. He wasn't delicate or sad though, he seemed almost sinister.

Antonio was trying to talk to him casually, his mustache moving cheerfully, when the man looked at Sebastian. His expression unglazed, and he looked at him, nearly smiling as if he recognized him. Something about it gripped his heart like he had felt that morning looking up at that mountain top. He was unexplainably afraid. Then the man began walking away. When he was about three yards away, before Antonio could say anything to him, he shrieked. He started shaking and grumbling, nearly falling. Antonio said something in Mixteco, and went to help him up, but the man stumbled away and began running, still grumbling.

There was some confusion as to whether they

should go after him, during which Sebastian stood still, his heart beating fast. The man disappeared around a curve in the road in a matter of seconds.

Antonio was the only one who was calm, finishing his drink while everyone else had lost their appetite.

A few minutes later, they were in the truck, growling up the road. The sun was level with them and as Sebastian sat watching it turn the clouds around it red. He was shaken, but was unsure as to why exactly. All he knew was that he didn't want to find that man. He barely had time to hope that he had disappeared, when they saw him up ahead, now walking on the side of the road.

As they approached him, Samuel slowed down and Sebastian could feel himself panicking. They drove up next to him, moving about as fast as he was walking and Antonio leaned out his window and said something. The man glanced up and then looked down as if in total misery.

"He doesn't want a ride?" Samuel asked.

Antonio leaned out the window again and said something. This time the man didn't even look up. He shook his head, "Just keep on going."

They moved on and left the man behind. But the feeling didn't leave Sebastian. The sun sank behind the clouds, and as the darkness crept into the truck, Antonio and the others were talking about what had happened.

"He must have a mental illness." Gabriel said.

"The people call him possessed," Antonio said, with no feeling or surprise in his voice.

Sebastian said nothing, but for the next few hours as they drove through the darkness, he listened to stories about demons and spiritual warfare. He had never heard such things, but they filled him with fear.

Wrapped in his sweatshirt, he hoped he would feel better when he got home. He was glad to see Vero and glad to receive a warm cup of sweet milk and a hearty dinner. But the night went on, and he didn't feel any better when he lay down on his twin bed.

He noticed the darkness again. And he couldn't take the picture of that man's eyes and the sound of the man's shouts from his mind.

Sleep. If he could just sleep, he thought. In the morning, it would all be better. But sleep only made it worse. He was awake in his dreams, tossing and turning between visions and memories. Fear gripped him by the throat. He wasn't sure if he was awake or asleep, but he longed for light, so much so that he began to think he saw morning coming through the cracks in the door, only to realize it was just another sick dream. He had visions of faces and eyes that he couldn't escape with eyes open or closed.

Finally, he was awake. He knew it. His skin was damp, and real light was just appearing, faded gray in the cracks of the doorway. He lingered in his bed, watching the gray light, free from the night at last.

Soon he sat up, and walked outside. He felt the cold air pass through his shorts and t-shirt and noticed the sky, covered in a deep blanket of clouds that hung very near above him. Ignoring the cold, he sat down on the bench near his door. The cold settled on his wet skin, but he somewhat enjoyed the sudden cold.

He was exhausted, he realized. What was he doing here? It's a terrible place... But though most of his thoughts were quiet, tired ones, he was deeply aware of something more than himself. It seemed to be in the air around him. It was the same thing that had tortured him in the night and it wasn't part of him. It infested the air, making it heavy.

Slowly he dragged his thoughts into the realization and acceptance of the things he had heard the day before. It was spiritual. This fear was not of himself.

The sun rose, turning the white clouds yellow. The day began and Sebastian had to continue despite the heavy air.

The sun made its way across the sky, despite the dread Sebastian felt toward the night. He stayed up late with Gabriel watching movies in the living room, but eventually it was time to go to his room alone. He sat on his bed alone with the Bible he had bought in front of him. It was time to think, it was time to decide.

"What, really, am I doing here?" he whispered to himself, "Am I just running away and surviving?"

He stood up and began pacing around the room, "These...spirits... this fear... it makes me want to leave." He stopped, "But if God had the power to save me in the middle of all this – in this place – He must have something for me here." He began pacing again, mumbling, "I saved myself, but now what do I do? Maybe I'm supposed to save others too. But that's silly, I don't know how to do that. If God could save me in the middle of all this, he can save everyone else too. But all this is for a reason." He sat down again. He realized he had a battle to fight, a very different one than anything else he had ever known. "I need to be here." he whispered, "He wants me here."

That night, the heaviness left him.

Chapter 13 – Calling

"What's it like to have a calling?" Sebastian asked while he and Gregorio were in the shop one day.

"It's something else," Gregorio mumbled, then looked up from his work realizing it was a serious question. "Oh, well," he sighed and put down his brush full of varnish, "I guess it's something that's different for everyone. The thing with me, at least, was that I wasn't so much concerned with saving souls, as much as I was just doing what God wants..." He began varnishing again, "It starts out just with salvation – being saved in and of its self is a calling, because we're called out and we give it all to God. But, I guess for some, it grows beyond that.

I guess what I'm saying is that a calling isn't always specific like we would like it to be. Sometimes it's just being where you know God wants you to be and doing what you can, even if it doesn't look like much." He looked up and held up his paint brush.

Sebastian smiled. "I'm glad to hear that." He went back to his work. The sand paper scratching at the wood, gliding smoothly under his hands. He sighed and stopping, glanced up at Gregorio again. "I've been thinking."

"Good for the brain." he mumbled.

Sebastian let his smile come and go, "I think I'm supposed to be here. I think I've been called."

Gregorio showed one of his rare smiles, "I have no doubt that your being here is no coincidence."

Something about telling a thought, seems to relieve

and confirm it in us. So, he was sure now, more than ever, that he was supposed to be there. He wasn't sure though, what he would do exactly. The fear was undeniable. He realized he was being illogical and stupid for feeling that he should stay in the poorest region of the country when there were so many opportunities for him elsewhere. He would probably always be poor. He didn't have much of a future.

He began to think that he couldn't live in Gregorio and Vero's guest room for the rest of this life. He had to find a permanent home.

One night, the family sat in their small living room with the television on, Vero curled up under Gregorio's arm, and Gabriel was buried in the pages of a book. Sebastian watched them, wondering at his own comfort as he sat with them. He almost felt guilty for feeling so at home. "I can't live here with you guys forever," he said during a commercial.

Vero snorted, and without opening her eyes,

mumbled, "Are you already getting tired of us, Sebastian?"

"No, of course not," he grinned, "Quite the contrary, I was just thinking... I think God wants me here, so I need to find a place to not inconvenience you."

Gregorio focused on him, "But how would you do such a thing? Frankly, I don't pay you hardly anything."

"Well, I have a savings account, and unless my parents have done something about it... it should still be there. It's a decent amount... I don't know, if I could find some land around here to buy, I could eventually, in a few years, build something on it."

"Land isn't cheap here. You would think it is, but it's not." Gregorio leaned forward and Gabriel looked over his book for a second. "We own this land," he paused, "But this isn't all of it. Our land goes down the hill to a creek down there somewhere. I tell you what, if you can find a decent place to build around there, go ahead."

Vero had opened her eyes when Gregorio had leaned

forward, but now she pulled him back and curled up under his arm again.

It was a crisp day, nearing the dry season. The rains were slowing down and soon would stop and not come back until next year. Sebastian started down the steep dry-pine-needle covered hill behind the outhouses. Pine trees poked up, long and skinny, with malnourished looking bark.

In a few minutes, Sebastian could hear the chattering of water and a few moments after that, the hill became less steep, finally flattening itself for a few yards until it hit the edge of the water.

Sebastian smiled. He made his way to the creek's edge and took a deep breath. It was a tiny little creek, with huge boulders towering high. It chattered along in some places and lay quietly under the roots of trees in other places.

He sat down on a bolder at the edge of the creek and

looked back on the semi-flat land. But as he mulled over how he would build something on that land, he noticed movement downstream. He was startled for a moment, having already accustomed himself to the sweet loneliness of the woods.

It was a young woman. He noticed right away her colored skirt and plain shirt. She didn't look up, watching the water as she slowly walked upstream toward him. As she came closer, he recognized her long, curly hair.

Rosalía was walking toward him slowly, her feet gliding from rock to rock. He wondered if he could move now and disappear up the hill before she noticed him. Just as he was about to make his move, she looked up and saw him. Her face changed and stiffened, but he noticed the moment before the stiffening that it had been soft and calm, like the pools of water under the roots of trees.

"Good afternoon," he said, and offered a casual

wave.

"Hi," she answered, "What are you doing here?"

He motioned for her to come closer and she looked at his hand and took one precise step. He smiled. "See that little bit of flattish land there?" he pointed with his thumb.

She nodded.

"I'm going to build a house there."

She looked at the land again and nodded. "So, you will live here?"

He nodded this time.

"What about your family?"

The smile faded from his face, "I guess... God's my family now."

She looked at him rather bluntly, her face motionless.

He gathered up a smile, "But that's the best kind of family, isn't it?"

"Here, everyone is related almost, so, we have family.

But, they don't really care that much. You and your brother seemed different. Very close, like you relied on each other."

"We did. Families, where I come from, are kind of like that..."

"Oh. Well, I guess families can be like that here too." she glanced away.

There was a moment of silence in which he watched the side of her face, "Is yours?"

She shuffled her feet uncomfortably.

"Oh, hey, how about we sit on that rock over there?" She looked worried as he walked a few feet away and pointed at a bolder. She walked to it and sat down, and he grinned, leaning against a mossy bolder a few feet away. "So, tell me about your family."

She looked down at her hands, "They're... well. My mom and dad are gone."

"Oh, that's too bad, I'm sorry."

She looked up calmly, "They aren't dead."

"Oh."

"My dad was from here, but my mom was from Ometepec, on the coast. I'm not sure how they met. He went to the United States right after I was born, and never came back. My mom stayed here for a while, but she left when I was three. They never really told me why she left me... but I think it's because she wanted to move on. You can't move on if you have a baby to remind you of the man that left you. Besides, another man would be less likely to take her if she had a baby. "She looked away over the water.

She didn't seem sad. Just quiet. She was strange he thought, as he watched her quietly looking away. Her nose was sloped perfectly, pointing delicately over the water. What was she thinking about so calmly?

"That's why you look different." he said.

She looked at him.

"I mean, you don't look like most of the girls here. It's because your mom wasn't from here."

"Yes. That's why." She let her eyes drift away from him again, "I don't remember them. I have a picture of my mom... she did look like me. But my dad didn't leave any trace of himself here except for me. He's my uncle's brother, so I guess they must look a little alike."

He hesitated, "Do you ever think of trying to find them?"

"Sometimes," she didn't seem to notice his hesitation, "It was a lot harder for me when I was little, but now I've realized that it's normal. So many other people have worse lives. My uncle feeds me and gives me a place to live... my cousins are like my brothers and sisters."

He wasn't sure whether she was indifferent or being thankful and optimistic. He couldn't read her. She seemed calm, yet indifferent, maybe angry or worried, but yet maybe she was just shy and didn't like him asking her so many personal questions. He realized, when he thought about it, that he really was asking her too much. "But it's not normal." he blurted out anyway.

She looked at him again, with frank and quiet eyes, "I'm not saying it's good, but that's the way people are."

"Not everyone."

Her eyes flickered for a second before she looked down at her hands.

"I'm sorry," he said slowly, "I shouldn't be asking you these things and telling you these things... I know how hard it must be for you and it's not right that I give my opinion without really knowing. But I promise you that not everyone is like that."

She looked up at him and a small smile formed on her face, "Thank you." She sighed and the stiffness seemed to leave, "It's hard sometimes. Family can be good, but when it's not, it hurts."

He looked at her in surprise. Her face was calm and soft, "Exactly," he said, "It hurts. I may never see my family again. I do know my mom and my dad... I love them very much. What hurts worse is that I know that this is my decision, I know I caused the division in my family."

"Did you?" Her eyes were wide and swimming in creamy brown, it was as if something in her burst open and she was finally there in front of him.

"Yes. I made the decision to be a Christian, even though my family doesn't want me to. I left home."

"Yes, but it was for God. If it was for God, then the fault is on God, and God can have no fault. Here, most of the Christians don't have Christian families. There are women that have husbands that will hurt them if they are a Christian, but they are one anyway. They do it for God because they love him. It hurts them, but it's for God. He causes a division between sin and Himself, so if sin hates us, maybe we're doing something right."

There she was, spilling out words like he couldn't have imagined her doing before. They were quiet, but true. He smiled, "You're right."

"Sometimes I think that God doesn't cure the pain,

He just gives us hope that it's not in vain. Hope is more beautiful than a cure... I guess God wants to make us beautiful things, not painless things."

"Wow..." he looked down, "What beautiful thoughts you have."

He looked up in time to see her turn pink, "I'm sorry," she said, "I talk too much."

"No," he laughed, "I'm the one that talks too much."

She looked up at the sky for a second, "I should go now." She got up from her hard seat, and held out her hand for Sebastian to shake it.

"That's fine." he smiled.

"Good luck with your house."

"Thank you. Do you come down here often?"

"Sometimes."

"Then maybe I'll see you again sometime."

She turned pink again, "Maybe."

He watched her move away briskly downstream. He

was wholly surprised, there was much more to that thin, Indian girl than he ever would have thought. He looked at the land and felt ashamed. Who was he to think he could help the people here? One young girl already proved to him that brilliance of thought that could exist in the Indian mind.

He sat down on the boulder where she had sat, humbled at his own ignorance of the ways of God. He knew very little. He looked up at the sky, turning pink like Rosalia's cheeks. He closed his eyes. What was this calling? It was not to teach... it was not even to help, it was simply to be. To be at God's disposal, to be in this place. Maybe he was being called to learn, not teach, to be ignored by everyone except God. Maybe that was enough.

With his decision made, he took his backpack and set out one early Friday morning with Gabriel at his side. They caught the truck to Tlapa, and Sebastian once more drank in the bliss of early morning with the cold wind in his face as he stood in the back of that truck with the world moving around him.

He didn't think much about Gabriel, who remained silent at his side, until they arrived in the hot city of Tlapa. They had to find their way on foot, and flag down taxis, and Gabriel took the lead. He knew his way around with perfect calm.

They got to the bank, where Sebastian, with sweaty hands withdrew, counted, and put in the backpack, all the money he had in his account. It was more than he had remembered it being. He stepped out of the bank, with Gabriel at his side, suddenly very worried about the amount he carried.

"Don't act like it's a big deal, Sebastian, or people will be more likely to notice." Gabriel said, "You're just a guy with a backpack."

Sebastian grinned at him, and he grinned back. "You're quite the kid aren't you, Gabriel?"

He flashed a big toothy smile at Sebastian.

Chapter 14 – Beautiful Things

Rosalía wasn't sure of what had just happened, but her cheeks were still warm. She couldn't recall ever talking to a man for that long - that hadn't been her cousin or uncle. She didn't know what to think, she never had thoughts like these before. Sebastian had seemed to burst into her mind, suddenly declaring his presence in her quiet mind and it wasn't so quiet anymore.

She went about her business, distracted. She did go down to that creek quite a lot, to get away to a quiet place, but now she wondered if she should go down there. She found a feeling she never had before, a magnetic-like desire to go there and see him again. She wanted to, but was it one of those wants that is wrong? Without a doubt, her head was spinning.

A few days passed. There came a quiet evening when there was nothing Rosalía had to do. Tía was holding the baby, swaying slightly on the wooden bed. She stood in the doorway of the kitchen watching her. Normally on days like these, Rosalía would go for a walk, avoiding the town and its people by going down to the creek.

She thought of Sebastian. If she went down there, maybe she would see him, yet again, maybe she wouldn't. But it shouldn't depend on that, should it? She should just do what she always did.

So, she set out on her walk, telling herself that she was just doing what she always did, besides, he probably wouldn't be there anyway.

She was right. When she got down to where she had seen him before, no one was there. The land where he said he wanted to build a house was untouched.

She sat down on the same boulder, realizing that she was disappointed. Then she felt silly for feeling disappointed, and angry at herself for feeling silly. Yet, she stayed there, looking at the semi-flat land, letting her thoughts wander over it in no specific direction.

As the sun disappeared behind the mountain top, she stood up and wandered away down the creek. She sighed, hoping that the silly feeling would leave with the sigh, but it didn't.

She had lots of time to sigh the feelings away because it was over a week until she went back to what had been her quiet place by the creek. She didn't expect anything this time, but strolled quietly as she always did.

He was there, though, looking at a slab of cement on the ground. She smiled, but tried not to smile too big. He grinned at her and she did smile too big. "Do you like my house?" he waved over the cement slab, "Please, come in for a cup of coffee." He stepped up on the slab and offered her his hand.

She hesitated for only a second, then took his hand for only the second it took to step up. The slab was about as big as the floor of the house where Rosalia lived, and even had the government *Vivir Mejor* stamp in the cement, but it looked a lot smaller because there were no walls.

"Right where we came in is the door. Over here, facing the creek is a window. I will put my bed next to it so when I wake up in the morning, I'll stand up and look out the window," he pretended to stretch and yawn. "Oh, but I offered you some coffee, didn't I? The table is over here."

She laughed as she watched him walking around his imaginary house. He grinned at her again, "You know," he said, pausing his tour, "I'd never heard you laugh before."

She laughed again, "Did you think I couldn't laugh?"

"Well, you always seem so quiet and..."

"Sad?"

"Well, yes." He pointed to the edge of the cement and they walked toward the edge. They sat down on the edge of the cement, on the part where the ground started to slope and therefore their seat was thicker cement.

There, with the creek trickling a few yards away, Rosalía answered, "I'm not sad. Sometimes I'm worried, though, and I just don't have any friends to make me laugh."

"Well, you have one now." he smiled, then took a breath, "Why don't you hang around the other girls of the church? There are some others around your age, right?"

"There are some girls, but they are younger than me and well...I don't like to go out much."

"More of the walking by the river type, huh?"

No, more of the avoiding people type, she thought, but just nodded.

"So, if they're all younger than you, does that mean that you've been going to church longer or does it mean you have started going just recently?"

"I've been going for a long time. I'm the oldest that goes now, because the ones that were around my age, most of them are all married now and don't go to church anymore."

"But how old are you?"

"17."

"So, young? They marry here, so young?"

"Yes." She didn't let him ask more but quickly changed the subject, "I've been going to the church meeting here since I was a kid."

Sebastian laughed, "Don't tell me you were one of those kids that hangs around here constantly?"

"I was. I think I was about seven when they first came here. I was one of those quiet, little girls who peaked around corners."

Sebastian laughed again, "I imagine it."

"I hung around them and went to church because well, they'd feed us and give us stuff. It was when I was about twelve, I think, that I started getting serious about what they were actually teaching us. I started coming to church not because of what I could get from them, but because they were talking about God."

He smiled at her and she felt her face turning red. She was sitting too close to him, she thought suddenly. But he didn't seem to notice anything, "That's really amazing. You were so young. I guess I never thought that one could become conscious of God so young, but I think it's wonderful. You have a head start on things. I mean, I'm just a baby in Christ... you have five years and I have five weeks."

She looked at him, feeling less shy, "Five weeks?"

"We all have to start sometime." He looked down for a moment, "We should do something with all the young people of the church sometime, don't you think?"

She watched him as he began to plan outings with the youth of the church. It was almost possible to see his mind working, quick and precise, like a well-oiled machine. She watched with wonder, amazed at this energetic mind before her that seemed so open and free. Before she knew it, she was responsible for inviting all the young members of the church that she could think of to go after church on Sunday to the basketball court.

She agreed with him, quietly, kind of afraid to actually do it.

"I really want to get to know the people at church, especially the young ones, because they are the ones that can make the most difference, but are most likely not to."

She left a while later, happily confused at this guy that was building a house by the river.

Next Sunday came along. When she walked into the pavilion, she spotted Sebastian sitting in front next to Gabriel. He saw her and waved, then nodded with a questioning look on his face. She nodded back, then found a girl or two to tell them that Sebastian wanted all the young people to go play basketball after church.

The other girls giggled, since Sebastian had become quite an interesting topic among them. Rosalía sighed, feeling sillier than ever. She hoped she could skip out on the basketball game as she hardly knew how to play anyway, and the girls could get Sebastian to themselves.

After church, she tried to slip away, even avoiding shaking everyone's hand but just the people who were between her and the door. But one of those people was Vero, who would not allow her to leave so quickly.

Before she had a good excuse to leave, Sebastian was next to her, grinning and wiggling his eyebrows, "You ready Rosa?"

She felt herself go pink. "I told them, and they're going, but... I don't think I can."

"Your Uncle won't let you?"

"I don't think– "

"I'll tell you what," he smiled, "I will go with you to

ask his permission."

She looked at him.

Finally, Vero chimed in, "Yes, Sebastian, that's a good idea." she smiled.

Without saying anything more, they made their way up the street, Sebastian following at her side. She didn't know what to say. She didn't want Sebastian at her house and she didn't want him to talk to Tío. Maybe Tío wouldn't be there, yet maybe he would be drunk. Her stomach turned.

The people in town were watching her. She could feel their eyes on her, walking next to the tall stranger. Suddenly, the stranger interrupted her thoughts, "Do you play much basketball?"

She saw him, smiling next to her and let her breath out, "I hardly ever play."

"Why not?"

"I'm busy I guess... I don't know, never thought much about it, I suppose. I probably won't play good at all."

"Oh, don't worry about that. I played in high school," he cupped a hand around his mouth, "I was terrible at it." he whispered.

He was so carefree, so happy, she couldn't help smiling. Then she felt sick, as they were getting closer to her house. They climbed the hill to her house and she remembered, he had been there before. They got to the top, near the open door, and she saw Tío coming out.

When Tío saw Rosalia, he started to say something— loudly—in Mixteco. She cringed, mostly out of embarrassment. In a flash, Sebastian was standing a little in front of her. She looked past half of his back to see Tío looking shocked for a second, but then approaching with a deep frown on his face. He looked up at Sebastian and the frown softened a little, but he didn't say anything.

"Sir, I've come to ask for your permission for your niece to go play basketball with me and some others from the church."

Tío eyed him suspiciously, that look Rosalía knew all too well, but still, said nothing. Instead, he directed his words to her. With his index finger extended, Tío began telling her, in Mixteco that she'd better not be up to no funny business. He began loudly, but when he glanced at Sebastian, his voice lowered.

Rosalía nodded. Sebastian put his hand out to Tío, but as if he hadn't seen him, Tío turned around to go back inside.

She turned to Sebastian and gave him the biggest fake grin she could manage, but for once, he didn't smile back. He was quiet on the way down the hill and when she glanced at him, there were two dimples between his eyebrows.

They walked in silence until he paused for a second on the dirt road, "Does your Uncle treat you good?" he cocked his head, his black eyes watching her closely.

She didn't know what to say. She looked at him,

waiting, but he wasn't saying anything else. He wanted an answer. "Of course, he doesn't." she turned and began walking again. The basketball court was in the center of town, still a long walk ahead. She walked quickly, not wanting to be asked more questions, but his long legs kept him at her side anyway.

"Forgive me, Rosalía." he said after a few minutes.

She didn't have anything to say, "Of course." she answered.

"I need to learn Mixteco."

"Yes. You need to, if you're going to stay here."

"Gabriel was trying to teach me some the other day and he taught me to say, 'I want tortillas'." He waited for a moment, "*Qubi yu shita.*"

She laughed.

"What? Did I say it wrong?"

"No, it just sounds funny coming from you."

When they arrived at the basketball court, Rosalía

somehow hoped it would be less awkward, but she knew she was wrong the moment they walked in under the tin-roof that covered the court. All the girls, especially, turned to look at them. She knew these girls, some of them very well, but it seemed as though they were seeing her for the first time.

"Rosalía's on my team," Sebastian announced with a smile.

The game began. She tried, but it didn't matter how much Sebastian passed her the ball, or even if he did say he was terrible. No one could be more terrible than her, she was convinced. It was an odd form of torture for her, but she kept trying. The game: 5 to 6, Sebastian passing her the ball with a quick tricky sweep behind him. It bounced off her head and they all laughed, except for Sebastian, who apologized fervently and insisted she get some free throws as a reward. With her head pounding, she shot three times with everyone watching her and missed every shot.

When the game was finally over, they started walking to their various homes. The sun was beginning to make its way to the mountains as Rosalía mixed herself in with the girls, hoping to fade away, only finding herself the center of attention. The other girls didn't care about her bad basketball skills, instead they whispered in her ear about Sebastian.

"It seems you've made a friend." Ignacia sung out in Rosalía's ear.

"Perhaps more than a friend?" Lucero giggled.

Her cheeks got hot. She glanced at Sebastian, who was walking with a very sweaty Gabriel at his side. He was watching her, dimples between his eyebrows.

Amalia watched her, "He cares for you." she said.

That night, lying in her bed she thought of Sebastian. He did care. It was a new thought, a new idea, but she couldn't help but hope a little.

Chapter 15 – A Promise

Alvaro Rubio Moreno stood looking at the remains of his opium poppy field. He looked down at the bright flowers crushed under soldier's boots. He walked through that field and then made his way across the mountain to his other field. It was still there, growing, but not yet blooming. Anticipating the arrival of soldiers, he had planted half his field in September and the other in December, knowing the soldiers probably wouldn't bother a field that still wasn't blooming.

After assessing the damage, Alvaro returned to his little house, having left it when hearing news that the soldiers were coming. His little house was empty and dirty since the recent death of his mother. His mother had been a little old lady whose death had long been awaited. She had been a tired old woman, but she had, like most mothers, sincere desires for her son. Of the seven children she had, he had been the only son in the family, born only a little while after his father left. No one knew for sure why his father left, but some believed he got crowded out by his six daughters and simply didn't care for a seventh. The little old woman wanted her only son to be important, and he was still trying to become the man his mother had wanted-- a man who walked through town with his head up, always having money in his pocket, but mostly a man that would have many sons after him.

For all the time that he could remember of his thirty years, he had gone to Culiacan, Sinaloa and sweated in the sun picking tomatoes. The worker's accommodations were bad and the work was hard, but year after year, it had provided for him and his mother. His sisters had long been sold and the money had been spent paying for their share of town fiestas by the time he was old enough to work.

On her death-bed, his mother told him, stretching out a wrinkled hand, "Get yourself a good wife, son, and have lots of sons so our family will be remembered in this town."

So, this was the year he had set out to do something to make the money to accomplish his mother's wishes and finally buy a girl, and not just any girl, but a good one. Young, and from a powerful family. But there were only two ways to make that much money. The first and best option was to go to the United States. He knew if he could make at least seven thousand dollars, he could come back and establish some sort of future for himself. But he ran into problems which had stopped him from trying to go. For one, he would have to borrow a lot of money to pay the *coyote*, and it was not sure that he would be able to pay it back. All would be lost if he was caught by the U.S. Border Patrol, or worse, if he died in the desert—many suspecting that is what had happened to his father.

So, he had settled for second best. He didn't have to borrow money to plant opium poppy and the only risk was the Army coming to chop down his crops.

He looked around his dark little house; with one field gone it would be a 40,000 peso loss. He found some money among the dusty things of the small house and walked to town with his head down. He entered the tiny store on the main street, and there she was, the girl of his dreams. Julisa wasn't 15 yet, but she was as beautiful as a ripe pear with creamy skin, and long, straight, black hair with a *fleco* of hair hanging over her forehead. She saw him and burst into a brilliant, big smile. His heart throbbed within him, but then it ached when he thought of the 40,000 lost and that he could only make, at best, another 40,000—only half the amount to pay the cost of the young Julisa.

In grouchy disappointment, he bought his beer and sat down with the other drinking men in the entrance of the store.

He looked miserably in the street where the children played and expensive girls and married women rushed past; where workers had begun to dig in the street in the process of paving the road. The other men would laugh and yell out to them in their drunkenness, but Alvaro sat silent and angry in his drunkenness.

His beers had already taken effect when he saw a girl he didn't recognize. She looked as old as 18, her skin sandy brown, and her hair wasn't oiled and wasn't cut with a *fleco*, but hung in long little curls. His eyes followed her as she hurried up the street, dodging holes and workers.

She would do.

Chapter 16 – Marks

It was a quiet evening, and for the first time in a long time, Rosalía was comfortable, happy and having allowed herself the luxury of hope. She was on her way up the hill to her house, smiling slightly. Everything was going to be fine, she thought. She would be turning eighteen in a few weeks and maybe things would get better. Tío wouldn't be so desperate to get money for her, and she could think about maybe doing something else with her life.

When she got to the top and saw Manuel leaning with his ear against the wall of the house, she smiled wide, "Hi Manuel!"

"Shh!" Manuel said waving her away.

"What are you doing?" she whispered, and came closer.

"Listening," he hissed back.

She leaned up against the board wall next to him. She recognized the voice of Tío immediately, but she never heard the other man's voice. It was low and sandy, like sand from a dark ocean.

"Tomorrow?" the dark voice said.

"As soon as she comes back." Tío answered.

"No, no," the sandy voice poured through the cracks in the wall, "first thing in the morning."

There was shuffling inside, Manuel started

panicking, "Get out of here," he hissed and started pulling Rosalía away.

"What were they talking about?" she asked, forgetting to whisper.

Manuel hushed her and pulled her around the corner of the house just as a man walked out of the house. Manuel slumped himself against the wall, looking casual, but hiding her around the corner behind him.

She caught a glimpse of the man with the sandy voice. He wasn't tall, he wasn't short, but probably a few centimeters taller than her. His skin was golden and bright, his hair thinner than normal. As he walked away, he glanced over at Manuel, "Good night," he said, as a greeting and a fair-well. He looked away and began making his way down the hill. He moved slowly, she noticed, and watched his silhouette disappear in the gathering darkness.

When he was gone, Manuel pulled her away from

the house a little way. He was breathing hard through his nose.

"Who was that?" she asked,

"That?" he looked at her with wide eyes and shouted in a whisper, "That is your husband."

She felt her insides fall to the ground and her skin get cold.

"He came about an hour ago to get you, but you weren't home. He's already paid and everything. You're his wife – he'll come first thing in the morning."

Rosalía hardly noticed the panic and rush in his voice, she hardly noticed anything except her own trembling.

Why now? Things were finally a little happy and there was finally hope for the future – but there never really was, was there? It was silly to think that God was actually going to give her something better than what was done in her culture. They were all right. She had been a naïve dreamer.

Her arms trembled as she hugged herself. Manuel was going on about this man that was her husband and she should have been listening. It was important that she know everything she could about him before he came for her, but her mind wouldn't focus on anything Manuel said.

"Sebastian!" Manuel said suddenly, and Rosalía looked up.

Realizing he wasn't there and not even knowing why Manuel had said his name, she shook her head fiercely, as if trying to shake him out of her head, "No, no," she covered her face with her hands, "Forget about him," she said more to herself than to Manuel.

She took a deep breath and began walking toward the door – "Where are you going?" Manuel grabbed her arm, "don't go inside! If you stay away and if you ask for help from your Christian friends, and Sebastian too, maybe they'll help you get away. You can leave and not come back."

She hadn't thought of it. Mexico City...Acapulco...
the world was so big... her heart skipped a beat then fell
flat, she sighed, "No, Manuel, I'm not running away."
She tried to pull away, but he didn't let go.

"I'm not going to let Alvaro have you."

"There's nothing you can do." He let go of her arm
and watched it fall limp at her side.

She turned to walk toward the house. "I'm not going
to give up that easily." He called after her. She looked
back and saw him turn away, almost running down the
hill.

She pushed him from her mind as she walked into
the house. Tío stood up from the table and started
undoing his belt. She stiffened, *No, no, please no.* He
must have known Manuel would warn her. She knew he
was getting ready to beat her into staying, to punish her
into obedience. She put up her hand, "Don't worry," she
said, seeing her hand trembling, "I'll go with him in the
morning."

He watched her with distrust. She knew he didn't believe her.

It was an odd thought that made her want to cry more than the pain did; all she could think as the belt stung her skin was that she should get used to it – this would be her life. Since she didn't struggle and her tears were quiet, Tío soon stopped, maybe believing her, or maybe feeling compassion. Rosalía didn't know or care, but it was over.

If it was belief, it wasn't belief enough for him to leave her alone. He put Irvin in charge of watching her closely that night. She wasn't even allowed to go to the outhouse without him outside. He mumbled curses about Manuel, but said very little to Rosalía.

Her skin stung and was beginning to numb when they sat down for dinner. It was quiet at the dinner table, too quiet. She wished someone would laugh, cry, anything... but the silence lingered on. She realized how little they cared. This is what it would be like when she was gone, but with another empty chair.

With Irvin following closely behind, she went to her bed and pulled out from under it the box where she kept her things: a hairbrush, a small collection of plastic earrings, a little plastic doll that was hers when she was little, and of course, her Bible. She found a corn sack under the bed and put her things in them, and then found her clothes, mostly draped over the rope across the room and put them in the bag, setting aside neatly the fresh skirt and shirt she planned to wear the next day.

She set the bag at the end of the bed and sat down, glancing at the red streaks on her arms as she did so. They felt numb. She touched them but didn't flinch, her arms weren't what hurt the most. Her shoulder and chest hurt the most, but she dared not look. She looked up and noticed Irvin was watching her.

"Do you want to sit down?" she patted the bed next

to her.

He shook his head.

"I'm not going to run away, you know that, don't you?"

He shrugged.

She sighed, "I'm going to miss you guys. Are you going to miss me?"

Irvin dropped his gaze, his boyish toughness turning into boyish sadness. He came and sat down at her side, not saying a word. It was then, for a split instant, that she felt a little less lonely.

Time dragged on, and finally she curled up next to the board wall, Irvin falling asleep beside her. The light off, she watched the glow of the fire in the kitchen, listening to the low hum of her family whispering in their beds. She closed her eyes, but didn't sleep. She looked for God behind her closed lids – but couldn't find Him. He was so quiet...but He was there. *Why?* She wanted to scream at Him, but didn't have the strength.

How could He just watch and not do anything?

She wanted to cry, but her eyes were dry. She didn't know if she was numb or paralyzed. Her sadness wasn't as strong as her fear. This was her last night of freedom. She didn't want to think about tomorrow night. *No, no, no...* God had to answer. But He was under no such obligation, was He?

She fell asleep from pure emotional fatigue, and slept deeply. The next thing she knew, light was barely touching the mountain tops. *First thing in the morning,* she remembered. But panic didn't grip her. She got up, not disturbing Irvin. She was tired and sad, but somehow, she felt her soul was at peace.

She went outside and in the early morning light, took a cold bucket bath. When she pulled off her shirt, she finally saw the extent of her bruises. The ones on her arms were only red streaks that didn't hurt to badly anymore, but across her shoulder and chest ran a purple line. She touched it, and wondered what her husband would think, or if he would think anything at all.

She dressed nicely and checked herself in the mirror on the wall. She didn't know what she was looking for, a change, a hint, a hope... but she just looked back at herself.

The sun was much too happy as it heaved itself over the mountains that morning. She had just begun to get breakfast when she heard Tia mumble from the doorway, "He's here."

Rosalia's heart leapt into her throat and suddenly it was beating very fast. She didn't know what to do. She heard Tío outside, "Your woman is inside." *Woman,* the panic that had left her in the night came back, but ten times faster. Then she saw him. He stood in the doorway. His hands were clasped in front of him. He had fixed his hair and worn a nice, clean, long sleeve shirt. For her.

Irvin brought her bag and she reached out for it, but Alvaro stepped in and took it from him, "Are you ready?" he asked her. The words struck her. The first thing he said to her.

"Yes." she answered, stooping to hug Irvin, and Teresa running up to join in on the hug. She stood up straight again, nodded at Tío and Tía, wanting so much to hold Mari for one last time. "Thank you," she told them and turned toward her husband. He grabbed her hand clumsily and lead her out the door.

At the bottom of the hill, he let go of her hand and started walking ahead of her, maintaining a pace of about three feet. She watched him ahead of her, observing his every movement in its slightest. Her heart pounded in her chest, her lungs working hard to take in oxygen.

They picked their way through the ruts and workers on the main street, then down a dusty road on the edge of town, until he finally stopped. In a few steps, she was at his side, "This is your home," he said, pointing at a little house under a tree down the side of the hill.

She followed him down and into the house. It was dark and dusty. A table against one wall, and a bed against the other. He set her bag down on the table and turned toward her, his eyes were brown and droopy as he looked at her, "This is your house now."

Chapter 17 – Noble

Manuel went straight to the carpenter shop where he thought he'd find Sebastian. He found, instead, Gregorio closing the doors for the night.

"Where's Sebastian?" Manuel asked him.

"He's down by the creek planning his house."

"Where is that?"

"Down the hill over there," Gregorio pointed toward the outhouses, "You can go straight down the hill or you can go around down that old logging road and make your way up the creek."

The words had hardly left his mouth, and Manuel was heading down behind the outhouses. Down the steep hill, he found the trail and at the end of it, he found Sebastian standing on his cement slab, looking around him, a pencil behind his ear and a notebook under his arm.

"Hi, Manuel! How are you?" Sebastian said when he saw him.

Manuel ignored the greeting and stopped a few feet from him, "It's Rosalía."

"Rosalía? What's wrong, is she ok?"

"She's been sold. He's going to go get her tomorrow."

At first, it struck Sebastian as odd; it must be a joke. "Are you serious, Manuel?"

Manuel nodded, eyes not clouded with pride or speculation; he'd never seen him so present and serious. He was horrified, "I never heard of such a thing!" He looked at Manuel, who looked back at him,

"No, wait. I have," remembering the thoughts of a different time in his life. "I got it." he snapped his fingers.

Sebastian's eyes were busy with thoughts as he rushed up the hill through the trees with Manuel behind him.

They rushed into Sebastian's room. He pulled a dusty suitcase out from under one of the two little beds, as Manuel looked around the little room.

He opened the suitcase. There were a few books and what looked like magazines inside. He began to flip through them, "I remember hearing last April that they approved it..." he mumbled. "And in June, it was published in the *Diario Official de la Federacion*[1]...Ah, here it is!" Sebastian couldn't help but feel exhilarated as he read out loud to Manuel: "'General Law to Prevent, Punish, and Eradicate the Crimes as Regards to the Slave Trade of People. Article 28: Punishment of 4-10

---

[1] The official publication of the new laws of the federal government. La Ley De Trata Humana (14th of June 2012)

280

years in prison and of 200 to 2000 pesos a day fine as well as the declaration of the annulment of marriage will be imposed upon the one who: (Section 1) Obligates a person to contract marriage without charge or in exchange for payment in money or payment in kind given to the parents, guardian, family or to any other person or group of people that exercise an authority over her.'" He looked up at Manuel from where he was on his knees, "Don't you understand? What— "he stopped and took a breath, "What your dad did is illegal." Manuel continued to look up at him. "'the slave trade of people...'," he trailed off, but Manuel only looked at him. "We have to go talk to your dad." He stood up.

"It wouldn't do any good. She's already been paid for. She's Alvaro's wife now."

He felt the excitement drain from his face, "But she's not with him yet?"

Manuel shook his head, "In the morning."

"Ok." Sebastian sat down on the edge of the bed, the *Diario Official de la Federacion* still in his hands. "What we have to do is go find this Alvaro and tell him." He stood up again, headed toward the door and opened it, "Where is this guy?"

"We should wait until the morning when he goes and gets her."

"Why? Let's go now and put an end to this." He looked outside, at the

gathering darkness, "Ok..." he put his forehead on the half open door. "First

thing in the morning. Early."

"Can I stay here?" Manuel said, looking at the bed on the other side of the

room.

"Sure."

Dinner that night was quiet. Gregorio and Vero looked concerned but had nothing to say about it, at first.

From time to time, Vero would sigh, "Oh Rosalía." Finally, Sebastian couldn't stand it anymore, "I don't understand how this could happen," he said, "They *sell* their daughters. I'm sorry Manuel but this is horrible!" Manuel didn't seem too bothered. While Sebastian had lost his appetite, he ate like it would be his last meal.

Gregorio cleared his throat and explained it all to Sebastian. His voice was tired as he explained the prices and ages and how they had been worried about Rosalía for a very long time. A heaviness sat itself down on Sebastian's shoulder, hearing what Gregorio said, "Sometimes it's voluntary, sometimes the girl likes him back and it's all dandy, but here it's not always like that. And Rosalía, well, she's a quiet girl, but I don't think she wants this for herself." He wondered what Rosalía was doing right then. He wanted to go promise her that it would be ok, that justice would prevail and he would help her. But would it be ok? *Don't make a promise you can't keep*, he thought.

"We need to get up before dawn," he told Manuel when they went into their room. He reached for the little alarm clock on the bedside table. Manuel just nodded.

Sebastian lay down on his bed, the little lamp still on, with the *Diario Official de la Federacion* in front of him. "Is the light bothering you?" he asked, noticing out of the corner of his eye Manuel also laying down but watching him.

"No. I'm ok."

"Ok."

"I knew you would do something to help Rosalía." Manuel said, "You like her?"

"I care for her well-being, yes." he caught Manuel smiling slightly and sighed, "besides, we need to fight against what is wrong, and this is wrong...Tell me, what is Alvaro like? Is he a decent man?"

Manuel shrugged, "I don't know."

"What do you mean? Don't you know him?"

"Not really. I knew of his family and where they lived, but nothing else."

"And what does Rosalía think of him?"

"I don't know. She knows less about him than I do."

Sebastian put down the *Diaro,* "Seriously?"

He nodded, "I don't think she's ever seen him before. She doesn't really go out much or have any friends."

"So, you're telling me that she's culturally bound to a man she doesn't know at all?"

He didn't say anything, only shrugged.

He groaned. He looked at the dents in the tin roof above him, "How was she when you left her? Was she happy, sad, worried?"

"Mmm... she was scared."

Now it was his turn not to respond. He turned out the light, "Goodnight Manuel, we have to get up not too long from now." But he didn't sleep. He wondered if Rosalía could sleep.

Sebastian woke up before the alarm went off. The sky was starting to turn gray. Careful not to wake Manuel, he got his nicest clothes and at the mirror in the outhouse, with gel, he made his hair as professional as possible. For once, he thought it was very important that he look like a city man, serious and professional.

It was about 7:45 when Sebastian shook Manuel awake. He had waited long enough, "We should get going, Manuel."

"It's too early..."

"Then, we'll wait for the guy to arrive. Justice doesn't sleep past 7:45."

"Who?"

"Oh, never mind, just hurry up."

While Manuel was getting ready, Sebastian peeked into the living room where he saw Vero sitting with her Bible in her lap, her eyes tired. Sebastian wondered if she had slept at all. "Excuse me, Vero, but can we borrow the truck? We'll get their faster."

"Of course, Sebastian. I'll get you the keys." she managed a smile.

He started the truck up and as Manuel was climbing in, he remembered something. He rushed into his room and picked up his backpack. He hesitated, thinking of the contents, but swung it over his shoulder.

It only took a few moments to arrive. Sebastian stopped on the road under the house, "Wait here," Manuel said, "I'll go see if he's here yet." The door slammed.

Sebastian waited only a few seconds before getting out, but when he made his way around the truck, Manuel was running down the hill, "She's gone!" Sebastian's heart dropped, "They just left. Let's go!"

He knew he was driving too fast, and he knew that he didn't know where he was going, especially now that they were going to pave the main drag, he had to take the back roads as Manuel pointed them out. "Do you know where we're going?" he shouted over the noise of the motor and his own breathing. Manuel answered something quietly and slowly, and he didn't understand.

"Right here!" he finally said.

The dust they left behind caught up with them when they stopped. He got out and waved the dust away from his face. He checked the backpack in his hand.

"This way," Manuel pointed and Sebastian began to follow him down the trail to the little house.

He took a breath. *Professional,* he thought, *don't show what you feel.*

The few seconds were eternal before the door finally opened. He glanced at the man who opened it, and then behind him standing in the middle of the room as if she had been placed there was Rosalía. He didn't let the melting relief leak onto his face, but he stood straight and began to give his previously thought out speech, taking from his backpack the legally documented proof of the illegality of this man's situation. Alvaro took the paper and began looking at it.

Sebastian saw Manuel rush by them and get inside. He watched Rosalía reach out and hug Manuel around the neck.

"I'm sorry, Sir," Alvaro said his voice calm and low, "This might have worked if you had come sooner, but I have already paid the money and there is nothing you can do. The deal is done. Maybe you should go stop the people who haven't done it yet." He sighed, "This girl is my wife now."

"I'm sorry, but this does not say that should make any difference. This marriage is not binding."

"Who says?"

"The law says."

"I know you mean well, but you're the only one that's trying to stop this. Go to the town authorities, and I think you'll be the one in jail." Alvaro handed back to him his law.

Sebastian looked past him to where Manuel and Rosalía where standing. Rosalia's face was drained and tired, and she looked so much older. He saw suddenly the beginning of the heavy age that came upon the young women of this town. He had seen it before in the eyes of very young women holding their babies.

"Rosalía wasn't your first choice." he said to Alvaro, "She deserves, at least, to be someone's first choice." His professionalism left him, and he glanced down at the backpack still in his hand, "I know how much you paid for her. Would you give her to me for double that amount?"

Alvaro's eyes grew wide when Sebastian opened his backpack and offered it to him. There it was, 80,000 pesos in cash--- his life's savings. He looked up at Sebastian, "What do I have to do for this?"

"Give Rosalía to me, and don't tell anyone where you got the money."

Alvaro nodded, looked nervously behind him at Rosalía, then back at Sebastian, "You have a deal," he reached for Sebastian's hand and then stopped, "I didn't touch her. She's fine."

Sebastian nodded and accepted his handshake, handing over the money, back pack and all. Alvaro took it, and turned to Rosalía, "Go with him," he said.

Rosalía looked at Sebastian with wide eyes, "Come on Rosalía!" Manuel took her bag with a big smile and walked with her out the door where Sebastian and Alvaro stood. Once outside, Alvaro took the backpack and went up the trail looking around to make sure no one was watching him. With Alvaro gone, Manuel laughed, "We can go home now!" He started to run up the trail.

Rosalia's eyes were still fixed on Sebastian, milk chocolate brown eyes sparkling with tears. "Why?" she nearly whispered, "How?... Sebastian." She looked away for a second, then turned back to him with the most tender, teary smile he had ever seen, "Does this mean I'm yours now?"

She really was beautiful. "Rosa, I... You are really

worth every penny of that money, and so much more, but I didn't take you from Alvaro to be mine. I want you to be free now, free to have your own thoughts, your own feelings, your own life. You are free now from everyone, including me." The smile left her face, but slowly she nodded. Her curls blew in a light wind and he noticed the marks appearing near her neck. He reached toward them, "Who did this to you?" His hand close to her neck, he watched the memories flash across her face. "That's all over with now, Rosa. Come," he reached for her hand, "Let's take you home."

They drove back to the church, slowly this time, with Rosalía in-between them. The day was beautiful and never had Sebastian known Rosalia's laugh to be quite as magical as in that short drive, as Manuel made her laugh and cry at the same time.

When they drove up to the church, Vero burst into tears and Gregorio into his rarest smile. "This will be home now, Rosa, for as long as you need it to be." Sebastian said, as they got out.

There were hugs all around, and Sebastian wasn't sure who was hugging who at one point.

"You did it Sebastian!" Vero said, holding Rosalía tight.

"How did it happen?" Gregorio asked, "Did he really just hand her over?"

Sebastian didn't have time to begin answering, when Manuel stepped in and told them the story, dramatized with his boyish expressions. When he told them about the money, Vero gasped, "Sebas... you gave him all your money?"

He nodded, "It had to be done. I mean, money comes and goes, but Rosalía is more important."

Vero began to cry again, "Sebastian Arroyo, that is the most beautiful thing, the most noble thing I've ever seen. You have such a beautiful heart."

Sebastian tried to shrug it away, suddenly

uncomfortable with the attention he was being given, "So," he said finally, "Rosalía needs a place to stay. I should find myself a new place to sleep."

"You can bunk with me," Gabriel, who had been quiet, but had joined in on the hugging, smiled.

He was ashamed of his feelings, after what Vero said about being noble, but as he moved his few possessions to Gabriel's room, he thought about his loss. He really had nothing now.

Chapter 18 – Freedom

26 de Marzo

Vero gave me this special notebook, bound like a book. She says it's for pretty thoughts, not school work.

I do have pretty thoughts now.

I am learning school now with Gabriel who learns at home with books. Sebastian has books too. He loaned us some. My birthday was a few days ago. That's when Vero gave me this special notebook and a dress covered in little pink flowers. Sebastian gave me a hug. No one uses dresses like this here, but I don't mind being different. I am free to be different.

My life changed twice in one day. I was in Alvaro's house just trying to breathe but, then Sebastian came. He took me away and saved me from that life by buying me back. He bought me not for himself, but for me. He wants me to be free.

Never have I known or seen so clearly, since I gave my heart to Jesus and believed in His love for me, something that so clearly showed me love.

I can't stop my heart now. I try to contemplate

and understand my new freedom as an opportunity to do all those things I've always wanted to do, but I don't want to be free without him – Sebastian. He has become part of all I want.

But I am learning what freedom is.

I want to give back to Sebastian what he gave. I want to find a way to help him build his house.

Rosalia

Chapter 19 – To Bring Him Back

On a quiet Sunday afternoon Drusilla Arroyo stood in her kitchen and with shaking manicured nails counted a small stack of bills.

"Drusilla!" The unmistakable voice of her husband bellowed out. She stuffed the stack back into her purse and turned to face her husband as he walked through the door.

"Yes, *cariño*?" she answered, her voice wavering.

He stopped in front of her, "We seem to be having a money problem."

"Oh?"

"Yes. What are your plans for that interesting little stack in your purse?"

"Oh, that. I was going shopping."

He sighed through his nose, "Don't lie to me. You've been giving him money, haven't you?"

"Giving who money? Who would I give money to?"

"I found some receipts, Drusilla, of quite large sums of money being deposited into a checking account in the name of Sebastian Arroyo."

"Oh, Draco! He is still our son!" She covered her face with her hands.

Draco put his hand up and she uncovered her face. He grabbed his wife's shoulders and looked her in the eyes, "My love, if you want to see our son again, don't pay him to stay away. If you want him to come home, you have to take away from him what's keeping him in those mountains."

"What do you mean?"

Draco smiled. "I'm the candidate for governor of the PRD, and for once I'm going to make a promise that I promise I'll keep. If we get the Evangelical's out of those mountains, our son will have to leave with them, or better yet, finally leave this new religion. It's a win, win situation. Not only will we get our son back, but we'll make the world a better place."

Drusilla nodded, close to tears, "I just want him home again."

Draco nodded, "Yes, and this religion problem among the Indians, must also come to an end. But the first step is to shut down that saving's account before he gets the money."

"He already did." Drusilla said, looking at the rug under her feet.

"What? When?"

"The last time I made a deposit, it was empty."

"Have you put money in since then?"

"A little."

"I'm going to take it out right now and shut it down." he sighed again. "How much money was in the account when he withdrew it?"

"A little more than 80,000 pesos..."

Oscar appeared in the doorway, "Wow Mama, that's enough to keep him away for a while."

Draco turned around, "Not if I do my part." He left the room.

She sighed when her husband left, and looked at her youngest son with a small smile that quickly disappeared, "Oh, Oscarito, we need to warn your brother. He doesn't have his phone anymore, apparently."

"We could call the *caseta* of the town."

Her eyes widened, "Do you have the number?"

Oscar's eyes sparkled at his mother, "I do."

Chapter 20 – Sawdust

It was good Sebastian didn't have much, because there wasn't much room in Gabriel's small room. Sebastian had the top bunk and not much else. Gabriel's room was small, yes, but only seemed smaller with Gabriel's various collections. Musical instruments and books were the more obvious collections, but a rock and feather collection were no less important to him, Sebastian soon found out. He also realized how overlooked Gabriel was because of his quietness, yet he was a complete person with a double culture.

Life went on, but now with Rosalía. Her family had found out about what had happened, but didn't want her back. She was free, and now lost, Sebastian thought. She spent most of her time with Vero, sitting in on Gabriel's homeschool classes.

Sebastian couldn't help but feel lost as well. He

thought he finally had some sort of plan, a future in this place, but now he was more cramped and awkward than ever.

He was in the carpenter shop when he heard a shout over the machinery, "They're calling your name on the loud speaker at the *caseta*," Vero shouted, "You have a phone call."

His heart pounded in his ears as he walked quickly down the streets. He knew of only one person who knew to call him there – Oscar.

His hands were shaking as he picked up the receiver, "Hello?"

"Hello Sebastian?" a slightly muffled voice answered.

He couldn't find his voice. It was his mother. "Mama?" he finally said, whispering past the lump in his throat.

There was a silence, followed by muffled sounds, then finally, her voice reached him again. "I... I miss you..." she said and took a deep breath, "You really

301

need to leave that place, not just for your own sake and ours, but for those people you're with. Your dad has been elected candidate, as you know, and if you don't come home, he's going to make sure that the Christians in those towns can't stay there anymore. You need to leave."

"What? But how is he going to do that?"

"He has connections in the Catholic Church. You know that Sebastian. It's important that you just back away from it all, **and** nothing will happen."

"Mama..."

"Oh Sebastian! You don't know what you're doing to me. You had so much potential. You were going to be a great man, a successful man. I respect your devotion to God, but Sebastian, come on. Be logical. You can't spend the rest of your life lost in those remote mountains. Be religious, be a Christian, but at least go somewhere else to be it."

He didn't remember hearing his mother talk to him

in that way, though she had many times to Oscar. He took a deep breath, realizing that he was the rebellious one now, and not just rebellious, but the son who was wasting his life. That was worse to his mother and he knew it.

"Oh Sebastian...just come back!" There was a hint of disgust in her voice and before he could answer, she hung up.

He walked back, slowly this time. He watched the sun throwing its light on the mountains. The kids were running and laughing on the half-paved street. He realized that they didn't watch him so much anymore. He had begun to blend in.

When he got back, lunch was on the table. Vero looked up excitedly when he came in, "Who was it Sebastian? Your family?"

He nodded, not wanting to say anymore.

He caught Rosalía watching him from her new place at the table. She looked concerned, so he tried to smile.

It wasn't until after dinner that night that he talked with Gregorio about what his mother had said, the part about his father and the Catholic Church. He didn't expect him to think too much of it. It seemed to be Gregorio's way to act serious, but never be worried. But that was not how Gregorio reacted. For the first time, Sebastian saw real fear fill his eyes, "This is bad, Sebastian, really bad. If they can get the Catholic Church against us, the whole town will be, and then the whole region will be, and not just us, but the local Christians too."

Gregorio looked down and said, "We need to hit the floor praying, but also...we need to brace ourselves." Gregorio didn't look him in the eyes, "I guess this couldn't last forever, could it?"

Suddenly it at all crashed in Sebastian's mind. It was his fault. He caused all of this. His mother was right – what was he doing here? And he thought he was called by God... he had done nothing but harm. All he had to show for his time there was Rosalia's freedom.

Rosalia's freedom...surely that was good. Surely that was of God. Surely God had used him in some way.

His days seemed endlessly long and useless. There were mornings when he wondered why he should get up. The day would contain nothing new, just more sawdust. The rainy season was approaching and with it, one year since he had come to this place with his brother. Since the phone call, he couldn't stop thinking about them, sometimes looking through his signal-less cell phone at old messages and pictures, wondering if he should call them. He didn't know what to tell them. He admitted to himself that he was afraid, afraid that with one phone call, he would undo everything, that one conversation could throw away his faith. Lying in the bunk above Gabriel, it would sometimes hit him, a deep homesickness. He missed his mother, his little brother, and even his dad.

Almost every night, they all watched the late-night news together. One night, Draco Arroyo, the new candidate of the PRD for governor, appeared at a podium. Everyone glanced at Sebastian, then back at the TV. Sebastian cringed.

Draco's voice was deep, resounding through the microphone as he made his speech. He made the news that night because of his out of the ordinary campaign promise. He expressed concern for the indigenous groups found in the state, proclaiming the urgent need to preserve their culture and ensuring that they are not disrupted or changed by any foreign power or belief system. The people in his audience cheered. The woman news anchor returned, stating that that was Draco Arroyo speaking on the necessity to preserve the indigenous culture in the state of Guerrero.

"Well, that's that," Gregorio said.

Vero put her hand on his knee, "Now, don't you start. He hasn't been elected yet."

"The PRD is always elected in this State."

"There's a first time for everything. Come on, we need to pray and tell the church to pray too. God isn't done here, Gregorio."

In the silence that followed, Sebastian fumbled with the strings on his sweatshirt.

"You look like him," Rosalía said quietly from the corner of the sofa where she sat.

Vero smiled, "It's true, you do look so much like him, and you talk like him too. You're both very handsome and well spoken."

"Thank you," he didn't smile, but stood up with a sigh, "Well, goodnight,"

"You're going to bed already, Sebas?"

"Yeah," he managed a smile, "I don't feel very good."

"I understand," she said, "Remember, we really love you. Don't blame yourself."

He tried to nod, looking at Gregorio.

Gregorio nodded at him, his eyes quiet.

He lay on his bunk, looking at the nails in the ceiling. He didn't know what kept him going. Some nights lying on his bunk bed, he wasn't even sure what kept him alive. He hoped it was God keeping him, maybe floating in mid-air, but keeping him none the less. He could hear their muffled voices in the living room. They were his family, he realized.

He was still awake when Gabriel came in and found the light on, "I thought you'd be asleep."

"I was too lazy to turn the light off."

Gabriel laughed. In a few minutes, Gabriel was ready for bed, so he turned the light off and crawled into the bottom bunk. They were both quiet, but they each knew the other wasn't asleep.

"Would your dad really have said that if you had never come here?" Gabriel finally asked.

"Maybe...probably not. I don't think he cared about the villages before we came here."

There was silence until Gabriel said, "So how will

they do it?"

Sebastian sighed, "He'd get the Catholic Church against you."

"The Catholic Church is already against us."

"Well, he would tell the priests that they can stir the people up against the evangelicals in order to drive them out of their towns without any fear of intervention from the government. They would get away with it completely and entirely."

"Oh." Gabriel said and after a moment of silence, he spoke into the darkness almost as if he was talking to himself, "I don't want to go back to Mexico City. I don't fit in there. I mean, maybe one day I'll leave this place, but I'd go somewhere else... not Mexico City. They don't understand me there."

Sebastian listened. He had never thought how hard it must be for him. He couldn't make promises about what a wonderful, comfortable future Gabriel would have to make him feel better, and he didn't tell him he was over-reacting either. He only listened, knowing that's all he could do and that's all Gabriel wanted. It was all Sebastian wanted, too, but he stayed quiet, feeling the emptiness.

"Good-night, Sebastian." Gabriel said finally. "You know, I always wanted a brother." he said. Sebastian smiled softly in the dark, "Good-night Gabriel." he said.

He didn't feel homesick that night when he drifted off to sleep.

In the next few days, Sebastian noticed them trying to cheer him up, Vero and Rosalía especially. Vero made him special dinners, and Rosalía would ask him a million questions about the books she was reading.

He'd watch her eyes sparkling, talking about some book in Gabriel's collection. She would ask him a question and he'd smile, "I don't know, I haven't read it."

Her joy was his comfort. She was there because of

him.

He was looking through his papers one day. He wished he could buy all the girls out of their sad lives. There was the paper, the law that was useless... if only the people would listen to it.

It dawned on him, standing there in the little room he shared with Gabriel: they didn't know. He can't change the lives of those who had already been sold, but maybe he could aid in prevention. Maybe if they knew that there was a law, that there was punishment, maybe they would think twice. Maybe...but what else could he do? He could go to Tlapa and file a complaint with the *Judiciales*. But you can't report a crime that isn't actively happening, can you? And, technically, he did pay for Rosalia, so what he did was a crime. But here, now...maybe if he spread the word, fear would stop them.

So, the next day, he took the law in hand and walked to the *presidencia,* hoping to find the town authorities. Everything was dusty, despite the almost finished main street on which no one was yet allowed to drive on. Even the people seemed dusty, quiet or otherwise, they were dusty too.

The *presidencia* was a huge building and quite impressive, except that it was full of empty rooms. There were remnants of Draco Arroyo posters on the walls outside, and the faded eyes of his father were watching him as he climbed up the steps to the big porch, looking around for someone who looked official.

People watched him, people with dusty, unbelieving eyes. He probably should have taken someone who could translate with him, he remembered, but it was too late now. A man sitting not far away was watching him closely. He stood, arms closed in front of him, skeptical, like everyone else. "Can I help you?"

Sebastian swallowed as he realized that he had forgotten to act official, "Yes, please." Fancy words, he begged of himself, fancy words, "I would like to talk to someone with respect to enforcing the law."

"That would be me." the man said, unsmiling.

"Ok, well," he fumbled through the papers in his hands. Saying 'ok' gave him away immediately as someone from the city, he knew, but he also realized that the whole town probably knew who he was by now. He cleared his throat, and held out a copy of the law to the man, "Sir, I have come to the realization that this law is not enforced here, and it needs to be."

The man looked at him closely and took the paper. He stood and read it, a process which took quite a while. Sebastian stood and watched the man's face, knowing that the rest of the town watched him.

"This is the law?" the man looked up, his face twisted.

He nodded, pointing at the official seal, "I think it's important that the people be aware, for their own good."

The man nodded slowly, "Yes."

By the time the shock had blown over, the law about

the selling of girls was taped on a dusty bulletin board on the presidency porch. Sebastian shook the man's hand, asking his name as well. "Don Emilio, at your service."

Sebastian smiled and turned again onto the dusty street. Granted, he hadn't saved the world, but one man listened and Article 28, Section 1 was now public for the town to read...if it cared to. It was good, he said to himself, it could be the beginning of a change.

He arrived back home to find no one in the carpenter shop. Well, it was early yet, maybe they were still eating breakfast. Good, he thought, since he hadn't eaten yet himself. But when he swung himself around the corner into the kitchen, it was empty. Odd. Then he spotted a note on the table, *Sebastian, we are at your house. Come down when you get home, there is breakfast.*

Your house? Breakfast on a slab of cement? Some picnic. He put his hands in his pockets, and made his way past the outhouse and down the hill, through the pines until he heard the sound of the creek – but there was another sound too. Was that a hammer?

Clearing the last pine, he saw the beginnings of a wooden frame on his cement slab. Vero was the first to see him and threw her hands into the air, "Surprise!"

They were all there, Vero and Gregorio, Gabriel, Rosalia, Manuel and even a few of the other younger guys that went to the church. He didn't know what to say, "Why are you doing this?"

"It was Rosalia's idea." he looked up to where Rosalía was, under a ladder, handing nails to Gregorio. She smiled a small pink smile.

"We're using the wood that we were going to use for the church – but who needs walls on a church? It's better in the open air!" he laughed that rare laugh, "Well, don't just stand there – get a hammer and help us!"

Sebastian was there in a moment, forgetting about

breakfast, though Vero didn't forget and soon was waving a foil-wrapped taco at him.

The women and most of the young guys had left when the sun had begun to set. Gregorio and Sebastian where picking up the tools and looking at the half-of-a-house frame when Manuel came and held out his hand for Sebastian to shake, "Are you leaving?"

He nodded.

"Don't leave yet, I'd like to talk to you." Manuel looked confused, then shrugged, leaning against a post as Sebastian finished up. "You should stay for dinner. You've been working hard." He plopped himself down on the edge of the cement, "Sit down, Manuel." Manuel lowered himself down next to Sebastian, but didn't say a word. "How's your family?"

"They're fine."

"I know, I mean, they know about Rosalía don't they?"

He nodded, "Alvaro went and bought another girl,

316

the daughter of the man who owns the big store in town. Everyone knew about it. They say that you stole Rosalía, and she's your wife now."

"What? You did explain?"

He nodded again, "But they don't believe it."

"I notice you come to church now."

"Yes. I come so I can see Rosalía. She's like my sister, even more than my sister is."

Sebastian smiled, "That's good. You know you can come see her any time you like, we don't own her now."

He shrugged and changed the subject, "You're going to have your house after all."

"Yeah," Sebastian said, "God has done something amazing for me. I'm really humbled, honestly, that they want me here...that God wants me here."

Manuel didn't say anything for a few moments, making Sebastian wonder if he had made it awkward, realizing that Manuel had never been very interested in God, then he said, "Why did you give up your house for her?"

"Because," Sebastian took a deep breath, "because I knew God wanted me to do it. Rosalía was more important than any house," he was quiet for a moment, "the night before we went to get Rosalía, you said that I loved her. In a way, you were right, but not in the way you think...in a different way. In the way that God loved us and gave his life for us."

"Is that why you didn't marry her?"

Sebastian was quiet for a moment, "Yes, that's one of the reasons. The Bible says that a husband should love his wife like Christ loves the Church. I would like to be that. I would like to have that in me, but I don't yet...love is more than the emotion and I need to know, really know that I really love her and it's really God...I don't think I'm ready yet. But that's not the only reason. I have to consider her. I set her free and that means she's free from me too."

"Is that what God is like?"

"What do you mean?"

"You set Rosalía free like you say God sets us free, but then does God set us free from Himself?"

"Well, yes and no, Manuel... technically, we are free already from God. We can do what we want, but when God really saves us, we don't want to be free from Him. We want to love Him. We have no other choice but to love Him."

"That doesn't seem fair, I mean to have no choice but to love Him. I mean, now one just has a new slave master."

"No, Manuel, I don't mean that we don't have a choice, but that we just naturally chose Him because... well, it's all about love. When God saves us, we're free, but we choose to follow Him because we love Him because of what He did for us. He's our master because once we've known Him, we want Him to have control of us, because we trust Him. We trust Him because He's proven that He loves us."

"So Rosalía might naturally love you because she trusts you because she's seen that you love her?"

"Our lives can't be compared with the things of God—not always. Sometimes it works out that way but sometimes it doesn't…"

Manuel didn't say anything more. Looking out at the dusk, Sebastian didn't know if he wanted to know about God, or if he was trying to figure out how Sebastian felt about his cousin. Manuel didn't seem the same as he did when he had helped him save Rosalía. There seemed to be something he wasn't telling him, yet, maybe he had told him. The town thought he had taken her from Alvaro, that she was his wife now. Maybe Manuel believed a part of the rumor. A knot gathered in Sebastian's gut. Surely, he didn't believe that. "Does Rosalía know about the rumors?" he asked finally.

"She knows about Alvaro."

"And the rest?"

"She doesn't know what they say about you, no."

"Don't tell her, please Manuel? It might hurt her."

Manuel nodded. In a few moments, he stood and said he should go home now. He didn't want to stay for dinner, thank you, and to tell Rosalía goodbye from him. With that, he was gone through the darkening woods.

They worked steadily for days, some days with more people, some days with less. They needed to get as much done as possible, to finish before the rainy season started, Gregorio said. Sebastian worked hard, enjoying somehow the tiredness of his muscles when he went to bed at night.

It was over two weeks later when the day finally came and the house was finished. Everyone was there that day. Even Antonio, the man that went with Samuel to the villages was there, as well as Samuel, who had come that week with his wife and daughter.

It was done, and he couldn't believe it, but what was more amazing to him was the people. They gathered in the kitchen that night, yawning, laughing, complaining about being sore from the work. They were so beautiful, Vero and Gregorio with their hands entwined on the table top, Samuel's smiling eyes and those of his plump wife and shy daughter, Rosalía, blossoming with everything good in her heart showing on her face. He knew in an instant that this was family. He wasn't homeless and he had a purpose, but more than that, he had the love of a new family. His heart was full and bursting and he didn't know how to thank them, nor how to thank God.

It didn't take him long to move in to his new little home, though he found it terribly empty and without a kitchen, but slowly he would finish it. That night he invited Vero, Gregorio, Gabriel and Rosalía to a little bonfire outside his house.

The sky was filled with stars – had he ever noticed? There they were, shining in hope and assurance of the God of miracles – the God that put him in that place at that time to be used in His way. He smiled, listening to his family talking in their own special ways around the fire. The fire cracked and the creek trickled, and their eyes sparkled in the firelight.

Rosalía was quiet that night, quieter than she'd been in a long time, but she smiled when Sebastian looked at her, so he knew she was fine.

It wasn't too late yet when Gregorio and Vero began to leave, Vero picking up trash and containers and leftovers from the feast she had brought down for the occasion. The others also began to leave, Gabriel following behind them.

"I want to talk to Sebastian about something," Rosalía said, "I'll be up there soon."

Vero glanced back, "Ok Rosalía, don't take too long."

"I won't"

"What do you want to talk to me about, Rosa?" he smiled, how pretty she looked, her curls dancing in the firelight.

"Oh... It's nothing. I just – "

"Are you ok Rosa? Is something wrong?"

"Oh, no. Everything's wonderful," she said as she smiled shyly and then looked down, then away at the fire. "I need to tell you..."

"Yes?"

"I love you."

Chapter 21 – Milky Way

She felt her insides flutter. She couldn't quite believe she had said it. She turned to watch Sebastian's face: had it blushed or turned pale? Or both? Is that possible?

"Rosalía..." he finally said, oh, her name on his lips sounded sweet, "You shouldn't say that." He took a step away and her heart dropped.

"Why not, if it's true?"

"Rosalía, I didn't save you so I could have you. When

I said you're free, I meant it. It's just God's way of giving you a better life. I'm not that life, I'm not meant to be for you."

"Why do you say that? What if God does want me to be for you?"

"No! He wants better things for you than me..."

"I think you're good."

He started pacing back and forth, "You don't know. You don't know what I'm really like and you don't know what other people can be like. There are good, godly, mature men out there that would be honored to be yours."

"But I don't know any of them."

"I know, but you need to. Go, Rosalía, explore the world." He put his hands on her shoulders and looked earnestly at her, "There are so many better people, better places, better everything. You need to know them. You need to see."

She felt her throat tighten, "But," she whispered,

knowing he could hear her, "But... I love you." She felt warm tears start to escape her eyes.

"Don't say that..." his voice came back in a whisper. "I don't deserve it."

Suddenly she felt angry, "You do deserve it!" she nearly shouted, "You deserve my love, but if you don't want it, I'm not going to force you. I want to see the world, but I wanted to see it with you. Forgive me for thinking you cared. Forgive me for saying I love you."

He had stepped away from her, his eyes so easy to read: surprise, sadness, regret. He was about to say something, but she didn't want to hear. She turned and left, not saying one word, though she heard him - and couldn't help but think how beautiful it sounded - calling her name.

She went quickly to her room, not wanting for Vero to see her tears and ask what it was about. There was a pain in her chest, and she let herself cry as her mind told her things, things that made her cry more. He didn't want her. She was foolish for imagining he liked her in that way, that he would accept her. He wanted her to leave, so she should and suddenly she wanted to. There was nothing for her without Sebastian, not in this place.

She fell asleep that night with her mind trying to think of better things, trying to imagine the day he would regret pushing her away, the day she would be happy, but despite her bitter thoughts, her heart was still in pain, suffering from its disillusion.

She heard his voice, and her eyes flew open. It was morning. His voice came again, muffled. He was outside, talking to someone.

Pulling the covers over her head and curling up tight, she decided she wasn't going outside. She didn't want to see him. She listened to her own heartbeat, aching, but fast.

Someone knocked on the door and she held her

breath, "Rosalía?" Vero's voice made its way through the wooden door.

"Yes?"

"Can I come in?"

"Yes." She sat up in bed, as Vero came in.

"Are you ok, Sweetie?" Vero touched her cheek pulling Rosalia's hair from her eyes, "He came and talked to me... He told me what happened, at least his side of it."

Her hands went to her face, "I shouldn't have told him I loved him." she said through her hands.

"Yeah, probably not." she heard a smile in Vero's voice, "But you were just being honest, saying what you felt... You're new to this."

"Oh, Vero, he doesn't like me. I made a fool of myself. He wants me to leave."

"Now, now, you know why he came up here this morning? He was worried about you. He doesn't want you to be hurt."

"It's too late..." she took her hands from her face, "I'm already hurt. He didn't do anything to me...he has only ever done good to me. But I gave him my heart and he gave it back to me."

Vero's eyes watched her sweetly, "Don't you see, Rosi? That's what love is."

"No, it's not." Rosalia moaned and buried her face into Vero's shoulder.

Vero rocked back and forth, in a way Rosalia imagined a mother doing, "I know it hurts sweetie...I know. Would you like me to give you my advice?" Rosalia made a vaguely compliant moan, and Vero continued, "I think you scared him a little by telling him how you felt. Some men might take advantage of your feelings, but Sebastian has been going through a lot of change and he has a tender heart right now. That's the reason that he rejected you right now, he's just not ready. Maybe in time, you will both be ready, or maybe it's not meant to be."

She took her face from Vero's shoulder. She didn't know what to say. She felt foolish and hurt, "Maybe I should leave," she finally said the thought that was nagging her so much.

Vero looked surprised, "But where would you go?"

"I don't know." she admitted.

She looked at her, worried. She never recalled seeing Vero very worried and it frightened her. "Well," Vero finally said, "We'll see. Right now, we should eat some breakfast and try to be happy… Ok?"

Rosalía nodded, reluctant to go outside.

Sebastian stood up from his chair when she walked into the kitchen, "Rosa," he said softly, "Could we talk?"

She glanced at Vero, who nodded, "I guess so."

The sun was hazy in the sky as they walked outside, "Let's sit down here," he motioned toward the wooden bench outside her room.

They sat about five inches away from each other,

Sebastian glancing at her every few seconds until he finally took a deep breath, "Last night didn't go well," he looked at her intently, but she refused to look back, "I didn't respond in the right way, I suppose I was just...just surprised."

"I know, I know..." she blew at a clump of hair that had fallen in front of her face, "I shouldn't have said that."

"But was it true?"

"It was the truest thing I've ever said." She finally glanced up at his face. There he was, his black eyes shining and caring like she had always known them. Her chest filled with a feeling, something like a mixture of love and pain, hope and fear. She didn't want to look away, she watched him as his thoughts crossed his eyes.

"Rosalía," oh how sweet her name sounded, "I...you are a wonderful girl. I don't want you to ever doubt that. You are sweet and kind and very...very beautiful."

Something sweet shot through her veins, never has anyone said that about her, "But," he said, the sweetness tangled up somewhere in her throat. Always a 'but', "I'm not ready. I can't..." he paused, his thoughts just out of her reach as he looked at her, "I am a new Christian, I don't have a plan for my future and... I want to see you well taken care of. I want to see you happy. Goodness, Rosalía, I like you, I do. But I can't...not now." he looked down at his shoes.

She noticed the little hairs on the back of his neck, he needed a haircut... he was breathing somehow out of pace with her, was he out of breath? She couldn't help but smile a little: he liked her. That was more than she had thought. "I understand, Sebastian."

"You do?"

"I do."

"I'm so sorry," he looked up at her again and reached for her hand, "I never want to hurt you."

His hand was rough, but held hers softly for a few

moments, then let go, "I know." she said when she found her voice again, "But, I'm not sorry for telling you. You need to know how much you mean to me."

"Thank you, Rosa." he said nearly in a whisper.

They sat quietly for a few minutes, then she noticed there was a little girl peeking around the corner watching them.

"I do want you to experience as much as possible, though," he said, "It would be good for you to see different places."

She nodded.

"Gregorio and them are going to Mexico City this summer to visit their family and they'll probably take you with them."

"That would be nice."

"It would... So, are we ok now Rosalia?"

"Yeah."

"You're not mad at me?"

"I could never be mad at you...Well, not for long."

He laughed, and it sounded wonderful.

She didn't forget him, but she didn't cry herself to sleep either. She loved him. That meant not doing anything at the moment. It meant caring like she always had. Needless to say, she wasn't exactly happy with the result of telling him her feelings. She wondered what would become of her, and worried about it, even though worrying about it hadn't done her any good in the past.

Soon, it was the beginning of June and election time. Everyone around her was on edge, worried she knew about whether Draco would win or not. Or as Gregorio said, "*When* he wins, if he'll go through on his promise." They tried not to talk that way in front of Sebastian. He was worried enough already. He tried to act like it didn't bother him, but Rosalia knew it did. It was his father, after all.

They gathered around the television as they always did, but didn't get comfortable. Sebastian watched with sad, quiet eyes, just waiting for the election results to be announced.

Then on the screen came the voice of a woman and the video of red, white and green balloons falling on a short fat man, the PRI won.

They stared blankly for a few moments. Gregorio's eyes grew wide and he turned to Sebastian, "The PRI won."

Sebastian's eyes showed a smile, then the screen changed and his smile dimmed, Draco Arroyo was in a sea of microphones. He was saying things; long words fast and angrily. He looked so unlike Sebastian, she thought, nothing like him.

The room seemed to erupt with talking and happiness. They didn't have to worry about getting kicked out of town. But Rosalía watched Sebastian. He seemed relieved, but not any happier than before. It was a great loss to his family. The Arroyo family would not be celebrating that night.

Sebastian left a few minutes later, and Rosalía followed him out. She found him outside looking up at the sky. It was clear and crisp that night.

"Hi Rosa." he said, without looking away from the sky.

"What are you looking at?"

"See there?" he pointed up, "That's the milky way. Well, the part of it we can see from earth." She looked where he was pointing, it looked like a line of haze or fog. "It's not a cloud." he said as if he had read her mind, "Not a cloud on a night like tonight."

Chapter 22 – Under One Sky

3 de Agosto

We got to Mexico D.F. two days ago. Close to the city, I saw snow on a mountain. Snow! But in the city, I could see nothing but endless lights and cars. It's amazing there can be that many people in one place. Gabriel says it's one of the most populated cities of the world, but he doesn't seem too excited to be here.

It's dirty even though everything is paved. It's colorful, the first thing I noticed driving in was the graffiti up in places that seem unreachable.

I've seen more of it now. It's big. Very big. I have seen how everything one could want to know, see or feel is in this city. It's so full of people, and so many different people. Gregorio said that on Sunday we will go to a church where the pastor is from France and his wife is from the United States. It is as if the whole world is under one sky in a place called the city of Mexico.

We went today to see some old buildings and Gabriel was telling me about the Mexican history that happened here. When I was in school the teacher would tell us to be proud of being

Mexican, I never really understood what that meant until I saw this city.

But I must say, I miss Sebastian. I wished we could explore the world together. I wonder if he thinks of me, I wonder if he thinks good things of me.

I try not to be angry, but I'm tired of being unwanted... I know it's not true, but it feels like it sometimes. I hope he misses me. Sebastian was right in a way, this city has opened my eyes to the possibility of living without him, but still, I don't want to have to.. I guess it's true what Vero says, I need to leave it in God's hands.

Rosalia

She closed her flower-covered notebook, smiling slightly as she tucked a picture in-between the pages. She opened it up again, thought a second, and made a note:

Gabriel took a picture of me in front of El Angel De La Independencia, he printed it out and gave it to me, and now I have it in this book for pretty thoughts. It's a pretty thought because I am in the city of Mexico under the statue of an angel of independence.

That Sunday, they went to the church Gregorio had told her about. He said that the pastor was a Frenchman who had been his friend since he was in the university. The Frenchman was a little older than him, and had come to Mexico City for some missionary purpose, but ended up being the pastor of this church. Rosalia didn't know what to expect when she saw these people.

The Frenchman fascinated her when she saw him, preaching at the pulpit. He rolled his r's with his throat, his blue eyes bulging. She was in awe of him and his slim, yet tall wife, and their church as well. The music was loud and the young men stood facing them as they sang.

One night, a few days later, as they readied themselves to go back to Cochoapa, the topic of Rosalia's future came up. They were sitting around in the living room of Gregorio's relatives, nice, but somewhat distant people, who had left them alone that evening.

She took a sip of a foamy coffee, a new and incredible thing that absolutely tickled her taste buds with its mixture of bitter and sweet. "Maybe you would be happy here," Vero said, "The people of the church would surely find a way; you could stay with someone and get some job here..." Her eyes were shining, but her words took Rosalía by surprise, their meaning frightening her.

"What kind of a job would that be?" Gregorio said, not smiling at all, "A maid? You know girls that get jobs here as maids usually don't end up very happy.

Besides," he looked at Rosalía, "I think God has more special things for her."

"She doesn't have to be a maid, *Gregorio;* she could help in the church. She's good with kids, she could do all kinds of things. God can use her here too."

Rosalía watched them, realizing they were arguing about her. She tried to interrupt, but it was Gregorio's turn to answer, "I'm not saying she can't, I'm just saying that I don't think she'd be very happy here."

"I think she would be, there are a lot more opportunities here. Back in Cochoapa, all she has to do is sit around and worry about Sebastian."

"She does more than that, you know that. You said she's good with kids and there are kids there too. There is a church there too, a church that needs much more help than the one here. Now Sebastian – "

Her cheeks burned hearing them talk about her feelings toward Sebastian, "Please stop." They both looked at her, "I...I don't know what I'm supposed to do with my life. The idea of having a choice is new to me. I do like it here, yet, I don't want to be alone here." She looked down, "Gregorio is right, I am not needed here – I would do the most good with my own people."

"Are you sure?" Vero looked at her, concerned and obviously disappointed. The look was not taken lightly by Rosalía, it struck her in a way that bothered her. Maybe she was wrong.

"For now," she answered.

Gregorio nodded, "You're right, you don't have to make those decisions right now. Mexico City will always be here."

Her coffee was less sweet, and everyone was quiet. She was worried suddenly, maybe this freedom wasn't all it was cracked up to be.

She went to bed that night, listening to the noise of the city. Didn't people sleep here? she wondered.

It was late and she couldn't sleep, this new worry pressing on her chest in the darkness. She was afraid suddenly, afraid of all the options, the places, the roads she could go down – roads that would never take her home again. And Sebastian… it had hurt her feelings that Vero thought she needed to get away from him, though maybe she was right. She didn't want to forget about him, not yet. She sighed, that was her problem…she didn't want to give him up. Didn't she trust God with her life? No…she was afraid that if she gave Sebastian to God, He would never give him back. Why did she want him back? What's the use of loving a man who doesn't love you back? She rolled over. They would be leaving tomorrow afternoon, so she should sleep. But she needed to trust God first, right? Why is trust so hard? Of course, God is trustworthy! He had done great things, hadn't He? If He did all those things, if she was sleepless in the city of Mexico that night because of Him and His blessings and grace, then why couldn't she believe that He'd keep doing great things? She pressed her eyes tight, as it was hard to pray that night... but she needed to get some things straight.

She got up and peaked outside the window. She craned her neck to see the sky, searching the black and orange-glowing sky for the Milky Way. She saw a red and blue light move across the sky. An airplane! But no stars...

Chapter 23 – The Sermon

He couldn't believe Gregorio thought he could do this. He looked down at his open Bible. The words were blurred, his eyes unfocused. He had a little less than a week to prepare a sermon for Sunday. He took a walk down the creek, read, wrote, took another walk and tore up what he had written. Are you supposed to write it down? The creek reminded him of Rosalía. He wasn't supposed to be thinking about her... yet, maybe thinking of her was exactly what he should do. He needed to preach to people that were very similar to her... that thought the same as her. This wasn't a professional speech. Her words echoed in his mind. *I love you.* Of course, love. Love is an attribute of God, but not only that, but about God being love in it's very form and what that meant for humans and how love should be in our lives.

If someone went and looked into a curtain-less and still glass-less window of a little wooden house by the creek, they would have seen Sebastian sitting at a wooden table that still smelled of cut pine, leaning over a Bible mumbling, "Love suffers long and is kind...never fails... by this we know love."

The light stayed on until late that night as he paced across the floor. He was no longer thinking about the people and how they needed to know what love was, he was convinced that he himself didn't know. It was so much more than he realized. You feel it, you do it, but you don't know it. There are perversions, realities, and truths that he had never realized were ever possible. It wasn't a romantic thing, like he had thought. It was so much bigger than that – so much more real.

Everything was based on love, and it was the one thing that would never go away.

He remembered that Samuel had once told him how the word didn't exist here. The sudden realization of the emptiness of their lives shocked him. Then he remembered Rosalía, standing there telling him she loved him, as if it was the simplest thing. It wasn't the simplest thing. She was using a word that didn't exist in her maternal language. She knew it was different, and she knew the power of those words more than he had.

He lay down on his bed, and listened to the creek outside, realizing suddenly that he had thought what she said wasn't that important. It was just a crush, he had thought. But she wasn't using love the way the girls in Acapulco would. She didn't love him like she loved her favorite color. When she said love, she meant it.

He didn't sleep well Saturday night, thinking about what he would say the next morning. He had studied and made his notes neatly, he had prayed about it over and over again, yet he worried. Who was he to preach a sermon about love? The people of the church were more qualified to preach to themselves. He knew it. And he realized, Gregorio had known it too, but he was preaching for himself, not just for the people.

That was his comforting thought when he stood up on Sunday morning. There had been no guitar that morning, and it made it more nervous going up without having heard the people singing.

Marcos, a fourteen-year-old with a large nose, had volunteered to be his translator and stood next to him, then looked at him, waiting for words to translate. He started, awkwardly at first, he knew, but he had begun. He did better though, after getting the hang of the back-and-forth translating, but mostly, he felt better when he started listening to himself. This sermon was for him more than for anyone else.

Old women shook his hand afterward, and he didn't understand everything, but he was beginning to understand the idea of what the people said. He smiled, realizing he learned most of it from the kids who hung around them all the time.

The sun was being covered by afternoon clouds as he watched most of the people leaving the church. A few of the young people and kids were hanging around still, talking among themselves.

He sat down on the step of the church. He sighed. It was over with and he was hungry now. Skipping breakfast wasn't a good idea.

"*Hola* Sebastian," a little voice said.

He looked up as a little girl smiled at him. It was Eugenia, one of the regular faces around here. She held a little peach out to him, "*Hola* Eugenia," he answered. She was the only one who didn't act shy with him anymore. She was about six years old, with a dusty face, big smiling eyes and no shoes. "Thank you." he took the peach and turned it around in his hands, "Are you sure you don't want it?"

She grinned and unwrapped another one from her shirt, "This one is for me." She sat down next to him and took a big bite out of the little hard fruit, "Do you miss them?"

He took a bite from his peach. It was dry and sour. "Yup."

"They'll come back. Rosalia too. I like her."

"Did you like my preaching?"

She smiled up at him. "Yes."

In a few minutes, she had run away with the last of the people, leaving him alone as the afternoon rain began. He watched it, a small smile on his lips. It was quiet and lonely, but it was a joyful little loneliness.

The day of their return, Sebastian lingered a lot. Stepping out of the carpenter shop, looking down the street, sighing to himself didn't make them come any faster, and when they did come, it was when he wasn't watching for them.

The impression she made, getting out of the truck, in jeans and a nice shirt, was one Sebastian wouldn't soon forget. She seemed much older, though he knew it had only been a little over a week. She looked up at him and smiled when he walked toward them. It was the same smile and he saw in it that she was tired.

"I missed all of you!" he said, reaching to hug Vero and shake Gregorio's hand, "I shake your hand with great respect, it is not easy to do what you do every week." As Gregorio laughed, he turned to Rosalía and reached out to hug her, "I missed you Rosa." he said.

He saw her blush happily and wondered if maybe he shouldn't have hugged her, but wanting so much to tell her how pretty she looked and how glad he felt when she was smiling.

The sun had set long ago, and they still sat around

the table, talking about their time in Mexico City and asking about how things went around there, on Sunday especially. Soon it was just Sebastian and Gregorio.

"I'm glad it went well." Gregorio said, "I'm going to have to check with the people and see if you get an A."

He laughed, "All right, well don't get your hopes up, I just hope I passed." He stood up and headed to the kitchen door, "It looks like everyone already went to bed. I'll see you tomorrow, then."

Gregorio nodded and Sebastian stepped out of the kitchen, heading towards his house. Nearing what was his old room and now was Rosalia's, he saw her sitting on the bench outside. He stopped near her and she looked up. "I thought you'd gone to bed already."

"I should. I'm tired...but I can't sleep." Her hair was tied up, but messy, spilling over its tied bounds, she wore a sweatshirt and a pair of soft pants with clouds on them.

"Those are nice pants," he grinned and sat down on

the bench.

She broke into a little laugh, "Vero liked them. Honestly, I think she's making me into the daughter she never had."

"That's sweet," he smiled.

The smile faded from her face, "It is."

"Are you ok?"

"Yeah... I am." She was quiet for a few seconds, then added, "Do you know she wanted to leave me there?"

"What? Really?"

"Yeah. I thought maybe you would agree."

"Why would I agree to that?" She shrugged slightly, "I don't want to get rid of you Rosalía, no one does. We all care for you very much and would be very sad without you."

"Thank you." she answered slowly. They sat quietly for a few minutes, "It's harder in Mexico City. I know it is. God seems harder to find... that sounds silly I know."

"No, it doesn't. I understand that. It's harder to feel

352

close to God in cities because they're so full of distractions. It doesn't mean He's not near. It's not hard for Him to be near in a place like that, it's just hard for us."

"Yeah. How do you know that?"

He shrugged, "I guess it's part of the reason I'm here."

"I was thinking... if you would help me with something, Sebastian."

"Of course, what is it?"

"Vero used to give Sunday school classes. When I was little, that's what I would come to. It's part of how I knew God... but, her Sunday school class grew up and she kept trying to help us as young people, and most of the young people that are here, are here because of her. She's had a hard time helping us as young people and because of that, they don't really do anything for the kids now. I was thinking that I would like to start Sunday school classes with the kids. I haven't told anyone yet... but would you help me?"

She looked at him, her brown eyes quiet as always, "That sounds great Rosalia!" He smiled largely, "I would love to help you. You just tell me what to do."

She smiled, "You like the idea?"

"Yes! I don't know why no one has thought of it before."

"Well they have – "

"It's just perfect Rosa."

"Could you tell Vero and Gregorio with me?" she asked shyly.

Sebastian laughed, "I will Rosa, even though I don't see why you should be shy, it's a wonderful thing."

He was right, of course, when they told them the next day, they loved the idea. Rosalía looked at Vero shyly, but Vero wasn't shy with her agreement. She was full of ideas suddenly, taking Rosalía to the storage room and rummaging through boxes of crafts set aside just for that purpose.

Sebastian watched from the doorway as Vero jabbered on. Rosalía looked back at him, clearly overwhelmed. He smiled. She shrugged. He laughed silently, *it'll be ok,* he mouthed. She nodded and smiled, turning back to Vero who insisted she had a Noah's ark story book somewhere around here.

The following Saturday afternoon, they sat down at the kitchen table to decide and plan what they would do at Sunday school the next morning.

Rosalía spread out her notebook, her Bible, and some pages from the box of crafts, and began to explain to him how she wanted to do it and what she wanted to be teaching. He watched her and listened, amazed at her ideas. They weren't childish in the least. She seemed to take simple teaching to deeper levels, yet make it interesting for kids. How she did it, he had no idea.

Sunday morning, he was there, helping herd the kids down the street to an empty little wooden house that belonged to one of the men that went to church, with Eugenia holding his hand and skipping alongside him, "Is it going to be fun, Sebastian?"

"It sure is."

The little house was dark and dirty, but smelled of fresh wood because of the new little chairs they had put in for the kids. There weren't enough chairs, but the kids didn't seem to care, being used to squatting and leaning and sitting on the ground anyway.

He listened intently as Rosalia spoke to the kids in Mixteco. He listened for the rising and falling of the tones in her voice, understanding some, but not all. It was semi-chaotic, especially when a little one would start crying and Sebastian would discover a child's need to simply be with its mother and have to take him to his mother in the meeting.

As the weeks passed, they got the hang of it and knew the way certain children were. Mateo needed to be with his mother or he would cry like his little heart was broken. Eugenia would only pay attention if she was next to Sebastian. Victor would get tired near the end and would cry until Rosalía picked him up and would then fall asleep with his head on her shoulder. Mauricio didn't like Sunday school, and would sneak into the adult meeting, which was ok after all.

Sebastian discovered that October was his favorite month. The rainy season had ended, leaving a bluer than blue sky and the mountains dressed in flowers. He had watched Rosalía, her quiet ways, learned how her mind worked, but amazed by so much more than that. She was beautiful, not only on the outside, but Sebastian had found her heart, and it was richly colored, sweetly clothed. She hadn't mentioned her feelings anymore. He wondered if she had changed her mind about him. He'd watch her on Sundays, with Victor asleep on her shoulder and consider asking her if she still loved him. But what would he say if she said yes? Or no? So, he let October end without saying anything. Though it was in October, on a quiet Sunday afternoon, alone in his little house that he realized that he loved her.

He watched her, spoke with her about everything else, wishing he could tell her. But no, it was too soon. No, she may have changed her mind.

It wasn't until Christmas, as melancholy once again set in on Sebastian, that he decided he needed to speak to her. It was his second Christmas there, and though the first had indeed been the worst for him, it happened again that he missed his family. He missed the Arroyo family's fancy Christmas Eve dinner, their tree and manger scene. He also knew that his year would not be as grand as last year. They wouldn't toast to the success of the new governor, or to their eldest son that would be finishing law school next year, but they would ignore his absence. He imagined his mother missing him, he wondered if she would try to call, and he considered calling her.

The Saturday before Christmas, as was routine, he and Rosalia were in the kitchen preparing for the Sunday school class for the next day. She told him her ideas to tell the Christmas story in a fun way, and then asked for his opinion.

He nodded, "It sounds good." She smiled and was about to say something when he cut her off, "Rosa?"

"Yes?"

"Do you..." he glanced down, bending the corners of one of the coloring pages.

"Yes?"

He glanced up, "Do you still love me?"

She turned red suddenly, and looked down at the bent corners of the coloring page, "Sebastian! I..." He watched her, looking down with her lips moving slightly, as if trying to form the right words first, but then she stopped. She looked up at him and took a deep breath, "Yes." she spit it out, her face reddening again.

He watched her, and she watched him, their eyes unmoving. She was afraid, he could tell and longed to reach for her and tell her she shouldn't be afraid of rejection anymore.

"Why do you ask?" she nearly whispered.

"We're meant to be together, Rosa."

She looked up at him, her eyes round.

"Yes, I mean it." He leaned across the table and reached for her hands, "If I wait until I'm perfect, until there will be no conflict or hardship, to love you – then it wouldn't be love at all.

I wish I could give you so much more, I wish I could assure you that a life together will always be happy. I can't Rosa. But I love you, and for some crazy reason, you love me," he paused, looking down at her soft hands in his, "It really surprised me when you told me you loved me, I was at a loss...I didn't think you meant it. But I know now that you did. I didn't think I could make anyone love me, much less someone like you, and yet I didn't make you love me and there you were...loving me." Her round eyes watched him, her hands slightly trembling in his, "I know you're afraid, Rosi, so am I, but I don't want to think of living without you. Would you consider me, Rosalia? I might not be the greatest, but I sure would try to be the best husband."

She pulled her hands from his and covered her face with them, "Oh, Sebastian."

He couldn't tell if she was crying or laughing, but he was up and around the table, kneeling beside her before she could say anything else, "Rosa," she took her hands from her face. "I know this is fast, maybe too soon, I know. But I've been praying about it. I've been praying about you for so long...all God hears about is how wonderful you are."

She choked out a laugh. Her eyes were wet, but not red, shinning like a lunar eclipse. "Oh Sebastian."

"I understand. You really should think about it. You can give me an answer next Christmas."

She laughed again, "You're crazy."

"I know. I really am. I'm sorry."

"Sebastian," she said and reached for his hand, "You don't let me finish."

"I'm so sorry – "

"Shh," she patted his hand, "I don't need to wait until next year. I love you now. I have since the day you saved me. I couldn't love anyone else."

She was soon in his arms, nearly lifted off the ground in a hug. She smelled like sandy peaches. He didn't know what that was, and he didn't care. He kissed her cheek and marveled to himself at its softness and at how she turned pink when he did it. "We should tell Gregorio and Vero."

"Wait," she said, "Wait a little while, ok?"

"Whatever you say." he waited, then added, *"Cariño."*

It was Christmas Eve, Rosalía's first one with them, and Vero was rushing around making her own little fancy dinner for them. It was a quiet, but happy night for them. Rosalia's eyes sparkled when she saw the little lights Vero had hung in the living room, and it made Sebastian smile. She was happy, this was the most she'd ever celebrated Christmas and now she had so much more to celebrate.

They sat in the kitchen, eating their fancy dinner. It had been a few days and they hadn't said anything yet. So, Rosalía cleared her throat, glancing at Sebastian and making him produce a giant smile, "Sebastian and I have an announcement."

"Oh?" Vero glanced at them smiling.

Rosalía looked at him and nodded, "Oh. Ok. Well," he took a deep breath, "Rosalía and I want to get married."

Gregorio didn't smile, he looked frankly, in shock. Vero was, for once, speechless.

It was Gabriel who grinned, "Seriously?"

"Wow! When did this happen?" Vero finally found

her voice, "I had no idea, Gregorio, did you? What are you planning on doing?" She went on, not waiting for the answers to her questions, seeming more nervous than excited. It made Sebastian nervous and Gregorio's serious silence worried him. He glanced at Rosalía. She was either too happy to care, or oblivious to it.

It was almost a relief when Gregorio asked to see him after dinner. While the others were in the living room, continuing the celebration, Sebastian sat in front of a very serious, but somehow tired Gregorio. "Sebastian," he sighed, "I knew Rosalía liked you, and I suspected that you liked her too. But to go from that, to marriage is a very big step. You might think that you're made for each other right now, but let's face it, she's just the only girl available to you within a hundred kilometers. Also, you two have had very different backgrounds and cultures. It is not recommended to marry into another culture. It will not be easy for either of you."

"I'm not desperate. Yes, she is the only girl available to me, maybe that's why I fell in love with her. And culture, yes, I know. But I already gave up a culture and yeah, we are very different but, that shouldn't..."

Gregorio's eyes softened a little, "I'm not saying it's impossible. I just want to make sure you've thought of that."

"Of course, I have..."

"Another thing, Sebastian." he took another deep breath, "We have known Rosalía really well since she was still a little girl. She's always been really special because we've seen how God has worked in her life...and you were part of that work, I know. It's just that, well, you're still kind of new in some ways. I know you had a life in Acapulco, and probably a lot of experience with women,"

He felt a knot form in his chest, "Gregorio – "

"Let me finish. I know you are a Christian and you have repented of things, but I will not give my blessing if

I have any doubts. Rosalía needs to be treated right, and I don't want your past to ever come near her."

He felt his eyes filling up, hurt feelings and shame tightened his throat. Gregorio watched him, and he could feel his eyes. He found his voice just as a tear escaped his eye, "I never want to hurt her. I know she deserves better than me. Gregorio, I was not a good person before, but don't think that I am not aware of it. Don't think that I skipped over a few things when I repented and changed. I have fought with guilt for a very long time, but honestly, there is nothing I can do about it. God had to forgive me and clean me up... Rosalía is a precious gift of God and well, I hope she'll forgive me too. I don't want to hurt her. I'm sorry Gregorio, I really am. I understand if you don't approve of me."

Gregorio watched him as he wiped his eyes, "No Sebastian. I do approve. I just..."

"I understand."

"I just had to talk to you. Marriage is serious." He looked down and let out a long sigh, "I'm sorry. I know your heart is in the right place. I know you want to follow God." He looked up at him, "I know you love her."

He nodded.

"Who am I to get in the way of great love?"

He smiled.

"You have my blessing and my prayers."

"Thank you."

"Do you know when you want to get married?"

"We haven't talked about it yet."

When they walked into the living room, Rosalía looked up, and there was worry in her eyes. He sat next to her, took her hand and smiled, "It's ok."

"Are you sure?" she whispered.

He nodded.

Chapter 24 – Green Glass

In the months that followed, there was much talking and planning. His sweet, curly-haired girlfriend listened to him as he told her everything about everything: His family, his education, his whole life before Cochoapa. She listened with her large brown eyes searching his face, but it was as if she'd heard it all before. They would walk around town, her hand in his, not caring what would be whispered about them. They talked about her uncle, how it was necessary to go see their families, and restore peace where it had been lost.

But not everything they talked about was so serious. Sometimes they would talk of things in little bits and pieces, and smiles in between thoughts. On some nights, they would sit outside her room and talk about the future. Shyly and sleepily, they would dream out the days when their lives would no longer be two separate things, but one. At some point, Vero would stick her head out a door signaling a good-night. He would always kiss Rosalía's cheek carefully, say goodnight, and wave to Vero goodnight.

He would walk home through the woods in a clear sort of daze, as if reality finally reached the point where it was unbelievably, truly beautiful.

It was early February when they decided, with Gregorio's smiling consent, and Vero's child-like clapping, the date they would be married. To each other, they agreed, that it was time to take the first step to reconcile with their families. An invitation to the wedding was in order.

He was cowardly, he knew. Rosalía was going to visit her aunt and uncle with just Manuel at her side, and here he was with a black-inked pen hovering over white paper:

9 de Febrero

Dear Mama,

It may seem odd, I know, for you to be getting a

letter from me, now, after all this time. I feel it necessary, though, for you to know because you are my mother. I'm writing to tell you news that's very important for me and I hope you will share in my joy.

There is no tactful way that I know in which to say this, so I shall put it simply. On the 15th of next month, I'm getting married. Her name is Rosalia Cordoba. She has no middle name and no second last name because she doesn't know her mother's last name. She will be 19 on the 14th of March, so we chose the day after her birthday as our wedding day. Our story is a sweet one that I hope someday to tell you in the fullest of detail. For now, all I am asking is that someday, we and our children be welcome in your house.

If you are willing and if it is at all possible, you are most certainly invited to the ceremony, which will be small. You can call me at any time at the number Oscar gave you. Please tell him and Dad that they are welcome any time and that I love them.

I am truly sorry for all that has happened in our

family.

I think of you often, and shall always pray for you.

I love you,

Your son,

Sebastián Miguel Arroyo Espinoza

P.S. Enclosed is a letter from Rosalía. I hope you will grow to love her as much as I have. You are surely welcome in her sweet heart.

He took Rosalia's letter in his hand. She had asked him to read it and make sure it was ok, so he unfolded the piece of paper. He smiled at her handwriting, noticing how perfectly she had tried to write, most likely having copied it several times:

7 de Febrero

Dear Señora Drusilla,

I'm afraid I don't know what I should call you, please tell me what you would most wish to be called.

I understand how this is surprising news to you, but I hope it makes you very glad as it makes me very glad.

Your son and I have known each other for two years almost. He has always been very dear to me, having been kind and wise and teaching me so many things. He saved me from marrying a man that would have treated me very wrongly, and for that, I am forever grateful. Even in my gratefulness and love for him, he never took advantage of my feelings. He always has done the right thing, even when he knew it wasn't what I wanted. I know God put him in my life to show me a whole new world, and he has done that already. Now, I hope to live in the new world with Sebastian as long as I live.

I love your son very much. Thank you for bringing him into the world. I will do my best always to take care of him and be a good wife. I hope, also, to be a good daughter-in-law to you.

I hope to meet you and your husband soon, as well as see Oscar again.

Yours,

Rosalia Cordoba

Her letter to his mother made him smile, but everything she did made him smile. He folded it neatly with his, and put it in an envelope with the address clearly written on the front. No return address...he didn't have one.

He left the letter on the little desk where he had written it. He looked at his watch. Rosalía and Manuel were going to come back here when they were done. It had only been half an hour. He stood and went to work on the little kitchen he was building on to his little house.

Another half an hour passed, what could take so long? His nerves began to turn into worry. His worry didn't last too long, because a few minutes later, Rosalía and Manuel appeared around the corner of the unfinished kitchen. "Sebastian!" Rosalía exclaimed with her eyes shining, "You should have come with me."

"Really? They were nice?"

"Very nice. They're coming to the wedding." she laughed a little, "They seemed a little confused. They thought we were already married. But I explained."

He watched her, turning to talk to Manuel, then smiling back at him. At times she seemed so much older than she was. Like a serious and wise mountain woman that had seen so many things, she would rather forget. Yet, at times like these, she was like a child, frail and innocent, unable to see evil. Sebastian never knew that wisdom and innocence could go hand in hand, but there it was, shining in Rosalía's young face.

A few days later, Sebastian was alone in Tlapa, mailing his letter and getting a few necessities, like a ring for his fiancé and himself. He went to a tiny little jewelry shop where the man behind the counter smiled behind round glasses and a beard. He rubbed his hands together when he heard what Sebastian was looking for, but stopped when he found out how much money he had. Still smiling, however, he inquired upon the size of the bride's finger. Sebastian produced a sliver of paper that he had wrapped around her finger, marking the exact place where she said it felt perfect.

It didn't take long. He picked a silver ring with a small stone the color of pine needles. The jeweler admitted, with a wrinkle on his nose that, no, it was not a real emerald, but simply colored glass. He held it in the palm of his hand, light catching in the dark, green glass. It looked tiny next to the silver band for himself. He smiled, thinking it was perfect.

Chapter 25 – The Sure Mercies

On the day before the wedding, Samuel Clarmont came with his family. His wife and daughter had come many times before, but they had come this time especially for the occasion. His wife, Elisabeth, was a soft woman with silver in her wavy, brown hair and pink in her cheeks. She was eager to talk with people, a quality which Vero took advantage of. It had been a long-standing debate to decide who their daughter looked like, and she had concluded that like most children, she looked like both her parents, resulting in simply looking like herself. Her name was Hope, called that by her parents, but to the others, she was Esperanza. She had hair color like the hair her father had lost, and pink cheeks like her mother. She was about the age of Gabriel, and like him, was free in smile, but quiet, often found lurking around corners. There was a rumor among the children of Cochoapa that she read books in English and wrote English in notebooks.

That afternoon before the wedding, the women gathered in Rosalia's room. She blushed from so much attention, and even more when Vero brought the dress she had married Gregorio in.

"Vero..." she said, "Why do you have it here?"

"Oh, I had it in Mexico City for years, but I brought

it here a few years ago in hopes that some girl here might have a shot at using it again."

It was, of course, much too long for Rosalía, but only slightly too big. Elisabeth was a good seamstress, and with her instruction and the fewest stitches possible, they made Vero's dress fit.

When it was done, Vero stood back and tears came to her eyes. "I thought I didn't have a daughter to pass it on to," she said, "but now I do."

Outside, Gregorio said to Samuel, "The women have gathered together in a sentimental, tearful ritual in which they teach the new bride their secrets."

Samuel laughed, then said, "Where's Sebastian?"

"Probably off enjoying his last day as a bachelor."

Samuel laughed again and shook his head, "That's not a good way for the pastor who's going to perform the ceremony to talk."

"Just joking around. Around here, there are so few real and decent weddings. Weddings here aren't funny at all, so when there's a good one, why not throw in a few bachelor jokes among friends?"

The morning of the wedding day, after a breakfast in which the bride and groom ate very little and glanced at each other like frightened children, the women gathered in Rosalia's room for another 'ritual' as Gregorio called it, and he, Sebastian, Gabriel, and Manuel gathered in Sebastian's house for a ritual that Gabriel named, "The Tying of the Tie Found in the Donated Clothes that Doesn't Stink Like Old Clothes Anymore Because We Washed It". It turned out that none of them knew how to tie a tie, even though Sebastian and Gregorio had done it several times.

"Gabriel, go get your mother." Gregorio finally said after the fifteenth attempt to tie the tie.

Vero came a few minutes later suppressing a laugh. She had Sebastian stand in front of the small mirror nailed to the wall, then she stood behind him and tied his tie. She then straightened it, told Sebastian that he looked handsome, smiled comically at Gregorio, and left.

Gregorio chuckled, "They're called helpmates for a reason." Then he took a deep breath, "Ok, you're ready. Are we ready? Oh, Gabriel, Manuel, start getting the church ready, ok?" They nodded and headed out the door. "And don't get your clothes dirty, you're the best men." he called after them, "We're really scrapping the bottom of the barrel if they're the best." He mumbled. "So," he turned to Sebastian, "Are you ok?"

"Yeah, I'm fine."

"You're nervous, aren't you?"

"Yeah, but happy." he blew a sigh out of his nose. "Hey, if I sit down, will it wrinkle my pants?"

"If I say yes, will you stand for the next three hours?"

"Probably."

"Sit down."

He sat down gently on one of his wooden chairs,

glancing around the room to make sure his house was in order. They had brought Rosalia's things to the house that morning and though it hadn't taken him long to put her clothes next to his on the shelf that he used as a closet, he didn't know how she would want it. Her little box with her Bible and other things sat on his desk unpacked. He sighed again, "Three hours is so long from now, why did we decide to have it so late? And why does it have to be so big and fancy?"

"You've been out of the city too long. Fifteen people, a white dress, and a red tie is not big or fancy."

Three hours later, he stood at the front of the church, looking breathless. The people looked at him with blank faces and he looked back at them. Then the music started, a CD someone had found, since Gabriel couldn't play guitar and be best man at the same time, though he had asked repeatedly why he couldn't. Vero was beaming with pride as she watched Eugenia, almost run up to the front, scattering some flowers that came from a potted plant that sat near the outhouse. Behind her came Victor, toddling up with a little wooden box that he handed to Gabriel. Then the little ring bearer didn't know what to do. His face turned into a giant frown. Then the eyes of everyone in the open little church moved down to the entrance where Rosalía stood. Victor stopped whimpering.

That was the moment that had long been waited for, when the groom saw the bride coming towards him in a white dress. Any thoughts that came or went from his mind were expressed by the one tear that appeared in his eye and made its way down his face as she walked toward him. She looked truly like an angel from another place, yet she did not. She was a magical version of her unchanged self.

Holding hands in front of the church, everyone watched. Her family and people from the church were stone-faced and curious at this odd ritual.

"'By this we know love'," Gregorio read, "'because He laid down His life for us. And we also ought to lay down our lives for the brethren.' 'Love suffers long and is kind; love does not envy; love does not parade itself, is not puffed up; does not behave rudely, does not seek its own, is not provoked, thinks no evil; does not rejoice in iniquity, but rejoices in truth; bears all things, believes all things, hopes all things, endures all things. Love never fails.'"

He preached a short sermon, not so much for the bride and groom, but for the people that watched them with their mouths hanging open. The bride and groom didn't seem to notice anyway, they simply stared at each other as if they were stargazing in each other's eyes.

When it came time to say their vows, neither of them could finish without tearing up. And the vows themselves spoke of incredible promises, things no one had ever promised in those mountains before.

There was a murmur when the rings were produced

from the little wooden box that Gabriel had. They slipped the rings onto each other's fingers, and Gregorio proclaimed that Sebastian could kiss her. A grin passed the best man's face, then the groom leaned in and gave her that kiss. The audience may have been awed at the display of emotion, but that kiss both taken and given was a secret the bride and groom shared, a kiss that Rosalía had saved for that day, for him and only him.

As the people gathered to eat together, *pozole* with *mole* for the occasion, Rosalía and Sebastian greeted their guests. Tío and Tía looked at Rosalía, smiling in front of them in that white dress, as if she was a stranger. Tío seemed shy, nervous, and almost apologetic with Rosalía as he offered her his congratulations and best wishes.

A surprise awaited Rosalía, though. She spotted her in the small crowd. Hardly recognizing her since the last time she had seen her, Paulina stood by with her baby in her arms.

"Paulina!" she reached out to hug her, "You came, and brought your baby. Can I?" she nodded and handed her the baby, "Oh she's beautiful."

Paulina nodded again, "Just a girl."

"I'm so glad you came."

"Yes." she looked around, "You got love."

"I did."

They walked to their home that evening, Rosalía's white dress gathering mud at the hem. She wandered around the little house with a little smile on her face, Sebastian following closely behind her telling her she could do whatever she wanted here with this or with that, and if she could think of something they would need. When they arrived at the box of her things on his desk, she started taking her Bible out to put it on the little shelf next to Sebastian's books.

"Actually," he said, stopping her, "I have a wedding-gift-slash-birthday-gift for you."

It was wrapped in lime green paper, and felt hard and heavy, she looked up at him in wonder, "What is it?"

"Why do people always ask that? Open it, Silly."

She peeled the tape back, making sure not to rip the paper. Under the paper appeared a nice little box and inside a Bible bound in soft, blue leather.

"I made sure it was the same version as your old one," he said, pointing at the spine, "and it's a pretty color. Oh, read the dedication."

To Rosalía Cordoba de Arroyo, my love forever.

"Do you like your new name?"

"I do."

They sat outside the house as the sun set, falling behind the mountains in radiant splendor, preforming its best colors for them. The creek, meters away from their new home, chattered to itself as it rushed away in search of deeper valleys. Rosalía wrapped her arms around him, and he kissed her forehead.

To Sebastian and Rosalía this was only the beginning, everything leading up and adding to this was just part of their love story. Despite their young fears and uncertain future, they held with them the blessing of love, never forgetting how really dear and miraculous it is. Their two souls were two of many who knew and tasted the sure, boundless mercy of God.

To Gregorio, Vero, Samuel and all the people that had spent their years in hope for God to move in this place, the things that had happened wouldn't be very significant until they were things that were looked back on. They would see the great victory, and that love and God were seen in the happenings among them.

And to the people like Manuel and his family, the display of this thing called love would never be forgotten. Women would have it in their secret thoughts, and little girls would hope for it. Men would wonder, some would fear, and little boys would watch their fathers.

But if these mountains could talk, they would say so much more. They would speak of the spiritual battles they had seen, in awe of the beauty of the light that was breaking into the darkness. They would whisper that in the dark, spiritual realm that moved among them, there was a deep sadness and anger for the control and the power that had been lost and given over to the one true God. Maybe soon, the depravity would crumble and so many enslaved souls would be freed. The demons raged in weakening anger, yet unable to go past the boundaries of protection around God's people.

There were battles on the horizon, troubles no one yet could imagine, but God was faithful then, and would be always.

Made in the USA
Monee, IL
07 April 2025

15361919R10225